The Vision of Stephen

THE VISION OF
STEPHEN

AN ELEGY

Lolah Burford

The Macmillan Company

NEW YORK • NEW YORK

Frontispiece and end-paper illustrations
by Bill Greer

Stephen's song, on pages 167–68, is "A Prayer" from
The Poem Book of the Gael, edited by Eleanor Hull.
Reprinted by permission of the literary estate of
Eleanor Hull and by Chatto and Windus Ltd.,
London.

The Macmillan Company
866 Third Avenue, New York, N.Y. 10022
Collier-Macmillan Canada Ltd., Toronto, Ontario

Library of Congress Catalog Card Number: 77-185142

FIRST PRINTING

Printed in the United States of America

DEDICATED TO MY FATHER,

Joseph Michael

Contents

Contents

The Writer
Speaks Directly to the Reader Who Has Not Read Bede

Ⅰ T SEEMED TO ME THAT IF ONE COULD RE-CREATE A PERSON FROM ANOTHER TIME, THEIR TEMPER OF MIND, THEIR SPIRIT, THAT THAT MIGHT BE A GOOD THING TO DO; AND hardly had I had this thought than the Stephen of this story walked into my mind. He was clearly from Northumbria (an Anglo-Saxon kingdom comprising the present-day English counties of Northumberland, Durham, and York), for only in that place at a particular time could such a person have existed, and after looking into the sparse historical records of the time, the principal source for our knowledge being Bede's *Ecclesiastical History of the English Nation*, it occurred to me that the time he best fitted was in the reign of Egfrith. As I pieced together the relationships of that family, parts here, parts there, the choice seemed inevitable, although I have had to do some violence to one historical date, that of the separation of Egfrith and his queen. I have no conscience about this, for history is a box of facts, truths, mirrors, lies, and simple mistakes. It is also an allegory from which we may learn things about ourselves through the acts of other persons in other times.

For a reason which I shall shortly explain, to re-create this period in any archaeological manner is not possible, and this I have not tried to do. After attending the Anglo-Saxon lectures of Dr. Stephen Joseph Herben at Bryn Mawr College more than one year, and reading both in that period and in the period of the ancient Irish civilisation (whose Golden Age, though beginning earlier, continued into the Seventh Century, which was Northumbria's) for my own pleasure since 1948, a sense of the temper of that mind emerges for me. It is my hope it may be worth the sharing. I have purposely played down the strangeness of language, translating, as it were. To do anything else would be inaccurate. Caedmon's song, for example, no longer exists in the Northumbrian dialect, but only in Alfred's later dialect, West Saxon. No secular writing has directly survived from that period, only the writings of the clergy, in Latin. The literature of the courts, which survived orally, was written down by other men much later in other dialects. But to give a sense of the language, as well as to show what happened to the kingdom of Northumbria, with its court and its churches, I have included as an epilogue a piece of Anglo-Saxon written by King Alfred. It is an impassioned plea for learning which should be known for itself, but in these days, when Anglo-Saxon is less studied, it is hardly ever read. And those readers who have never seen an example of the language from which their own has descended may be interested in tracing the similarities and the differences through the interlinear translation.

Let me introduce briefly to those who are not acquainted with it this kingdom of Northumbria in the Seventh Century, highly cultured, now elusive, and therefore fascinating in the glimpses of it left to us. Settled by the Angles c. A.D. 500, who pushed back or absorbed the native British, it was originally divided into two separate kingdoms: Bernicia (the Northern, extending to the river Tyne and sometimes to the river Tees) and Deira (the Southern, extending to the river Humber), each with its separate royal city and its line of kings who gradually become interrelated as the balance of power shifts between the two, back and forth, through a tumultuous history of union, disunion, and a final union, before the dissolution. This settlement of the Angles occurs after the building of the Roman Wall by the Tyne River, and after the departure of the Roman forces from Britain. A brief glimpse of what they must have looked like comes to us in the story of Pope Gregory the First, which Bede recounts from traditional authority, and which I will paraphrase and partly quote from the first chapter of the second book of the *History*.

According to report, somewhere between A.D. 560 and 596 (when Augustine is sent to Britain), Pope Gregory sees certain boys in the marketplace of Rome, set out to be sold. He is struck by their looks, "of clear white skin and lovely countenance and also remarkably beautiful hair." He inquires about them and is told they are from the island of Britain "whose inhabitants are of such appearance." Asking, he learns that they are pagan still. He is saddened that "the author of darkness should possess men of such shining loveliness." He inquires the name of their race, and is told they are called Angles (*Angli*). "They are well called, for they have an angel's face, and such ought to be co-heirs of the angels in heaven." He inquires the name of the province from which they have been brought, and is told it is Deira. "They are well called Deirans [*Deiri*], being plucked out of the ire, the wrath of God, and called to the mercy of Christ." He asks the name of the king, and is told Aella, and plays upon the word "Alleluia"; "It is fitting that the praise of God the Creator must be sung in those parts." Sometime after this resolve he is able to send a mission to Britain, and later through King Edwin into Northumbria.

It is in the reign of this King Edwin, A.D. 617–633, a particularly winning king both in nature and ability, that for the first time virtually all England comes under one rule. Kent, the only kingdom of the seven not to acknowledge him as overlord, is nevertheless bound to him through his marriage. It is at this time that it is said, "A woman with her infant in her arms might walk from sea to sea without harm." Edwin is known for his ceremony, his standard of purple and gold, for his care for travellers and for roads, as well as for admitting Christianity.

It is Oswald, however, who calls in Aidan, monk of Hy (Iona), to be Bishop of Lindisfarne, the northern island monastery where the *Lindisfarne Gospels* were illuminated at the end of the century. Oswald, unlike Edwin, is of the house of Bernicia. A king of great sweetness and strength, he unites the two provinces or kingdoms of Northumbria again into one, and is killed in 642 by Penda of Mercia at Heavenfield near the Roman Wall. His relics afterwards work miracles; he becomes the first English saint. It is Oswald who took the silver dish from which he was about to eat and gave both the food and the dish broken into pieces to certain poor in the street come to request alms. The heathen king, Penda of Mercia, over-lord of southern England and slayer of five kings, was a legend in his own time; both he and his descendants will figure in Stephen's story.

With the coming of Christianity, particularly from Ireland, then known throughout Europe for its high culture, art, and learning, and for its adventurous sailors, Northumbria flowers quickly. Almost all our knowledge of the period, however, comes through the Church, and of the social life we have only glimpses, of kings and nobles, thanes and soldiers—and of others, nothing. However, Wilfrid, Bishop of York, who lived through the reigns of Egfrith and his successor, in his worldliness and energy suggests something of it. It is Wilfrid who encourages Egfrith's wife in her unwifeliness, who makes seventy journeys to Rome as only a small part of his active life, who builds large stone churches with French glass and marble, who lives and entertains luxuriantly to the point where he is criticised by the ascetic Irish Christian monks of Lindisfarne. Wilfrid officially brings Northumbria under the direction of Rome again, but just as the pagan and the Christian continue to coexist, so the Irish Church and the Roman Church continue unofficially to coexist and dispute. This Wilfrid, it might be said before passing on, is so little loved by Egfrith and his second queen that in addition to depriving him of his see in 680, Egfrith imprisons him for some nine months in a dungeon below a castle. Nor is he loved any better by Aldfrith, of whom we will speak more in his place in time, successor to Egfrith; Aldfrith will not receive him. Wilfrid, although not mentioned by name, will be mentioned briefly in the Ninth Division of Stephen's story.

Oswiu, Oswald's brother, after a period of internal conflict and division in Northumbria, succeeds to the throne. His children who concern us are Egfrith, legitimate, and Aldfrith, illegitimate, whose mother is said in Irish records to have been an Irish princess of Meath. It is Egfrith, self-willed and powerful, who is the king of my story, to whom I have given a son he is not known to have possessed. The records here are curiously blank and will allow it. But it is Aldfrith, the scholar-king, whom Stephen is most like, and I have cast suspicion upon him, even as I have cast a slander on the too much protested virginity of Egfrith's first queen who leaves him for the convent. These slanders, not provable, not disprovable, are not impossible, and not implausible; their justification is Stephen's insistence on a place in which to be born. I find myself half believing them; they fall easily into place, and they explain much that is unexplained.

Of Egfrith's life before he becomes king we know almost nothing, except that when young he was sent by his father as a hostage to Penda's court. Oswiu dies late in life, after a long reign; his most remarkable acts are to have slain Penda in 655, and to have Christianized Mercia. Egfrith's older brother mysteriously disappears from history, leaving rumours. Egfrith becomes king in 670 and rules until 685, overlord not only of Northumbria and Mercia but of the Irish of Argyll and the Britons of Strathclyde as well. He has received a large kingdom with troubles on its Northern and Southern borders, and for a time maintains and increases it; but after the battle of 674 against Penda's son, who has returned to power, Egfrith's character undergoes a violent change that is revealed by his actions in history. It is in the months before that battle in the autumn of 674 that the story written in this book takes place. After this battle (in which I have suggested the actual death of Penda's son Wulfhere which may have occurred instead shortly afterwards), Egfrith becomes more ruthless, more reckless, more bloody, and totally uninclined to advice, in both Church and state affairs. He ravages Ireland, "which is harmless and has done him no hurt," devastating the kingdom of Meath in particular, destroying churches and monasteries, for which he is much censured. The Irish curse him in his invasion, unable to do anything else, and when he dies, the curse is said to have taken effect and the Church holds out concern for his soul. He wreaks havoc on Scotland, and against the advice of his counselors and friends, proceeds on a reckless expedition against the Scots (the Picts) in which he and nearly all his men are slain, at Nechtanesmere, May 20, 685. A saint in Northumbria has a vision of his death at its hour.

The boundaries of Northumbria are now much reduced, the kingdom is pressed on all sides, and Mercia is again in ascendancy. With the death of Egfrith the period of the great Northumbrian kings ends, and never quite reaches the same high mark again. Bede is aware of this: he speaks of the glory beginning to retreat then "like an ebbing tide." And yet Bede is writing these words after the death of Aldfrith, in the age we look on as Northumbria's highest in culture and scholarship, when Jarrow and York continued to be, as they had been, the centers of learning and literature for all Western Europe. The court of Aldfrith was renowned, and the *Beowulf* poet may have composed the epic there. We consider this period of Northumbria's Golden Age to have extended for some years beyond Bede's life, but it is interesting that

Bede himself did not. For Bede, the ebbing glory began after Egfrith's death. It is worth considering why he may have thought this. Just before the end of the Seventh Century we have a civilisation combining the virtues of the nominally Christian warrior king–liege king with his liege thanes, and the Christian scholar—the Angle and the Latinist, but not in the same person. Stephen of this story, born of both, is torn between the two, and cannot reconcile them.

For a time under Aldfrith, who succeeds Egfrith without explanation, Egfrith having no son to succeed him at his death in 685, the two are united. He restores the kingdom in part, within narrowed boundaries, and "now reigns peacefully." This king, illegitimate son of Oswiu, raised away from Northumbria by churchmen and exiled by his brother for a time, has lived more in Ireland then in England before he becomes king and is known for his talk and for his silk cloaks of exquisite workmanship. After Aldfrith's death in 705 a scholar-king will not reappear for nearly two hundred years, not until Alfred, warrior and scholar without peer. But Alfred will speak and write in his own voice, and he will be the first of the English kings to do so whose words survive; all else earlier is shadows and hearsay.

Nevertheless, after the death of Aldfrith, whose reign is internally disturbed by politics but externally free of war, Bede has certain strange and startlingly prophetic words to say. One might expect him, as a monk, to welcome the change he describes, but as a realist, he apparently recognised the need for a strong state to protect the security of the Church. In 731, four years before his own death, as he closes his *Ecclesiastical History of the English Nation* at Jarrow in Northumbria, he writes this description, a muted warning, of the state of affairs he has observed:

And in the pleasant peace and serenity of the times, many Northumbrians, noblemen as well as private persons, laying away their arms, are eager rather for themselves and for their children to take the tonsure and subscribe to monasterial vows than to practise warlike pursuits. And what end will come of this custom, the next age shall see.

The next age does see, and quickly, before the century is out: Lindisfarne is sacked and burned in 793 by the Northmen, after frightening weather ("immense whirlwinds and flashes of lightning and flying dragons in the air") and then famine appear (*Anglo-Saxon Chronicle*). The monks are driven out naked, slaughtered, drowned, or taken away as slaves, altars are torn out and church treasures are carried away (*Simeon of Durham*). The scholar-monk Alcuin witnesses a "bloody rain" at York as a portent of the disaster, and worse to come. The next year Jarrow, Bede's monastery, is sacked. In 867, Northumbria is wholly destroyed by these Northmen, the Danes. With the taking of York, the traditional seat of King and Church, and the ravaging of Whitby, Caedmon's abbey (where I have placed Stephen), the glory that was Northumbria is only a memory, and hardly that. Sweeping from the North Sea downwards, waves of Danish invasions hit Northumbria hardest, most frequently, and most completely of all the English or Irish kingdoms. They leave nothing above the ground—as with Carthage, stone is not left upon stone, and wood is burned. Except in fragments and inferences the kingdom of Northumbria ceases to exist.

We know it did exist, and from certain evidences we may infer, as from the tip of an iceberg, what it was like, but that is about all. A few coins, out of the tradition of the king as "ring-giver," dated tentatively in Egfrith's and Aldfrith's reigns have been found; they are supposed to have been used for convenience in foreign trade rather than within the realm. In the end, the glimpses of social life afforded by the literatures of and about the time, in England and in Ireland, have appeared to lead where archaeology follows hesitantly when it can, confirming. In this century there has been the finding of the ceremonial burial ship at Sutton Hoo on the southeast coast of England, dated c. 655, earlier than Egfrith's reign. In the ship there are no coins but there are the remains of a small harp, along with the ornamented personal weapons, adornments, and treasures of the king, whose remains are not in the ship. But we knew already about the harp; Bede himself in passing has told us of it, in Caedmon's story.

This then is Stephen's world, summarised. As for the magic in this story, a reader of our century may ask, is there any justification for it? Perhaps. The Seventh Century was a time of pagan magic in the less civilised parts of the country, and of Christian miracles in the Church, and of occasional direct and material answers to prayer. It was an age in which mind and prayer frequently prevailed over matter. Witness the story which the factual and authentic Bede, a true historian careful of his sources, records without a blink: A young soldier-thane of Egfrith, captured and sold into slavery in London, could not be bound in any way, his fetters always loosening and falling off him. And why? Because his brother, a priest in Northumbria, thinking him dead, has been praying for his release from Purgatory. Bede has talked to the thane Imma himself. And if the Angles, as Christians, accepted magic, it was the lifeblood and breath of the Irish, who were also present in Northumbria.

It was also a time when Christianity existed in its simplest meaning and promise: that the world one knew was not the end, that one went from it into another. A haunting story is told by Bede of the taking of the Isle of Wight, off the southern coast of England, still British and still un-Christianized, in the year 686. The West Saxon king massacres all the native inhabitants of the island, except for two young boys, brothers of the king there. They escape across the sea and think to hide "from the face of the king," but they are betrayed in England to the English king and are to be put to death. A priest, however, seeing them, begs time to instruct them and lead them into the Christian faith, which is granted him. Moved by his words, baptised and made secure of eternal life, we are told, the boys submit joyfully then to the knife. It is our wish, reading the story (Bk. IV, chap. XVI), that those boys not die at all, but it is not Bede's.

But the transition from the Seventh Century to the year 1822? Why not 1821 or 1823? In 1822 the line from Shelley quoted in the story has been published, and it is the year of Shelley's death. There is no other reason, except that it was also a more peaceful, civilised time in England than previous years, and before the Victorian Age settled down upon the country. It seemed a good year. Our age would call in an authority. No age, however, seems golden to those living in it. I have put Stephen in this other age because in studying primary sources I have discovered that it is exactly the obvious things that people in a later age wish to know that people in their own age omit to speak of to one another for the very reason that they are obvious and need no speaking of. To speak of them at all I needed a contrast. I have also put him there because the story wished to fall that way, and in the end that is the reason. It has been said that all ages coexist in the relative and eternal time of God's eye. Let Shelley comment:

> I dare not guess; but in this life
> Of error, ignorance, and strife,
> Where nothing is, but all things seem,
> And we the shadows of the dream,
>
> It is a modest creed, and yet
> Pleasant if one considers it,
> To own that death itself must be,
> Like all the rest, a mockery.
>
> That garden sweet, that lady fair,
> And all sweet shapes and odours there,
> In truth have never pass'd away:
> 'Tis we, 'tis ours, are changed! not they.
>
> For love, and beauty, and delight,
> There is no death nor change; their might
> Exceeds our organs, which endure
> No light, being themselves obscure.

— 1820

The Vision of Stephen

Prologue

"Neque unquam prorsus ex quo Brittaniam petierunt Angli, feliciora fuere tempora; dum et fortissimos Christianosque habentes reges cunctis barbaris nationibus essent terrori . . ."

BAEDAE HISTORIA ECCLESIASTICA GENTIS ANGLORUM, IV, ii: Bede's *Ecclesiastical History of the English Nation*, completed in the year A.D. 731 at the monastery of Jarrow in Northumbria, in this passage describing the year A.D. 669.

And there truly have not been at any time, since the English first sought out Britain, any times more happy or more blessed; when both having most strong and valiant Christian kings, they were a terror to all barbarous nations . . .

The First Division

"IF YOU CONTINUE RIDING IN THAT DIRECTION," A VOICE
ALARMINGLY CLOSE SAID ALMOST IN STEPHEN'S EAR, "AS
YOU ARE NOW, YOU WILL RIDE INTO MORE TROUBLE THAN
you may wish for, Prince of Deira."

Stephen reined in his horse, on the first words of the
voice, and sat peering intently into the gloom of the forest
about him, trying in vain to search it out. He could see
nothing, skilled as he was in woodscraft, and now that the
voice had ceased, he heard nothing.

"Who are you," he asked without fear in his voice,
"and where are you, and for that matter, where am I?"

The voice chuckled, again alarmingly near him. Then,
without a twig breaking, the shadows moved to his left,
and a horse and rider showed themselves. He could not
believe it. He had looked there and he had seen nothing,
so still they had sat, so at one with their surroundings.

"I have set an ambuscade for you, young Prince, and
you will shortly fall in it, if you ride even twelve yards

further, and then I cannot help you. Do not speak or turn your horse, but ride him backwards, twelve paces, and then turn, and I will join you at the broken oak."

He had no reason to trust the voice, or the rider who owned it, but he did, and he followed the instructions of the voice exactly. When he came to the oak that had been broken in the thunderstorm of the spring before, but yet continued to grow, he stopped his horse and waited. Again he did not hear the other rider, but he sensed he was no longer alone, and that someone had come up behind him. His heart suddenly beat fast, wondering if he had ridden into a trap after all, but he did not turn his head, or move. The other rider slipped quietly into the place beside him, again materializing rather than riding into it. He had never seen such skill, and he had thought he knew the best.

"You are brave, Prince of Deira," the voice said, "and younger than I thought, and you have been in a graver danger than you might imagine. It was when I saw how young you are that I decided I would warn you and spoil my well-set plans. You have been very foolish, young Prince, and foolishness deserves its fate, but I have a special place in my heart for the downy chicks, and King Aella has none."

"I have crossed the line, I think," said Stephen, beginning to understand.

"You have indeed, but you are back across it now, though that may not save you, since you are so far from your home. If anyone approaches, I shall take your bridle in my hand, and say you are my personal prisoner. Then you must do exactly as I say, or we will both be lost, I as well as you. I may be merciful, but you will find there are no others like me, and you are a rare prize, Prince Downy-chick. What, by the way, is your name?"

"My name is Stephen," Stephen said, looking at his befriender with interest. He was not more than three years older than Stephen himself, for all his talk about the downy youth, but his face seemed older and sterner, perhaps because of his darker hair and complexion. He was dressed in the mottled colours of the woods, and he wore no insignia of any rank or band. He caught Stephen's scrutinising gaze and smiled wryly.

"I wear no marks like you, my Prince; no fillets to shine in the forest for me, to lure the hunters out."

"Who are you?" asked Stephen.

"Let us say I am a fighting man of Aella's. That is true, and to leave it there is best. I have not taken care you should not know me to tell you now."

A faint suspicion stirred in Stephen's mind, but he found it hard to credit.

"What were you doing in our part of the forest?" asked his semi-captor, for Stephen knew his motions lay at the other's wish. "Were you merely foolish, or had you business there? I have been watching you for three days now, and each day you have gone deeper. Are you spying out our land?"

"I am merely foolish. I have been following a white deer, and each day I lost it, near this oak. In the excitement, I forgot that I was near the line."

"I believe you. That is my deer. I raised it from a fawn. Would you have shot it?"

"No; I had heard there was one. I wanted to see one. I never have, though I have heard the stories."

"Then you shall see it now. You shall have something for your pains and for the danger you are not yet out of." He gave a low call, half-voiced, half-whistled, and then he repeated it. After a few moments, in which the strange young rider motioned Stephen to be very quiet, the undergrowth parted, and a white doe, great with young, appeared in the clearing. She came delicately over to the rider in the mottled green, and sniffed his hand and nuzzled at it, and then she approached Stephen, who watched her come in sudden ecstasy.

"Be absolutely still. The stag is over there, beyond the trees, and if you move or threaten her, he will charge you. I told you, our side is full of perils."

Following the other's eyes, Stephen could just see the pale branching horns, and the dim pale shape, looming enormous, larger than any deer he had ever laid his eyes on.

"Heart of my heart," said the other boy softly to the doe, "go back now to your lord, and let us leave this spot." The doe, raising its head, and sniffing the air, seemed to salute, and then stepped swiftly off to join the other deer.

A look of alarm came suddenly into his eyes. "God of storms defend us, I have waited too long, with these silly deer. Take that all-betraying fillet off your head, Stephen mine, and give me your bridle and do not speak. We shall bluff our way out yet." He had heard the approaching sound long before Stephen's own ears made it out, and he took a horn from his pocket and blew three certain notes and then three more in quick succession.

He turned to Stephen. "You are memorizing it, but it is wasted effort. Since you have heard it, I shall change it, of course, tomorrow." He then shouted to the other man, who approached, before he could speak.

"The prisoner's mine, and the spoils are only mine. I did not need you, as you see, and I shall bring him in myself. Go tell the others to stand off, and meet me at the hall."

"Now," he said to Stephen in a low voice, "you must just trust me. Help me to help you, and I will, fool that I am. We shall follow them, sedately and discreetly, and let them lengthen out the distance between us. When that is done, as soon as some tree or rock hides us, I will smack your horse upon his hinderparts and you, for your part, set him in a canter. I shall follow straight behind you. Go south, straight down the hill, towards the Spring of Freia, you know which I mean? We will meet there, and make our parting, or if you need direction, I will give it to you there. Be easy, Prince, it should work out."

Some breathless moments later, both horses drew up by the Spring of Freia, a beautiful spring, wild and ferny and fresh-springing with clear water, but they did not notice it, except to drink thirstily and to water their horses. Their flanks were heaving, and the two boys sat down on the stones that bordered the spring.

"How old are you, Stephen?" his companion asked.

"I am fifteen. I shall be sixteen in December, on St. Stephen's Day."

"I thought as much, but you look even younger. Neither your king nor mine will care, though, to spare an enemy because he is young, and certainly not a young viper to grow large. I do not know why we should fight. Do you?"

Stephen shook his head. "I do not indeed. It seems the way we live."

"Your father means to attack us. It surprises you that I know that. He is bent on making all this land beyond the Tyne his again. He may be right to want to do it, perhaps he is, but we have an ancient tradition and an ancient lineage to our land of Bernicia, as ancient and by us as cherished as yours by you, and we wish no part of your land. We want only what is ours. Could you not tell him this?"

"I could tell him, but he has his vision, and men of vision will do much to achieve their visions that may not be kind. He would not love me for it, if I told him."

"Kings seem much alike," the other remarked. "They are set in their separate visions. But the young, perhaps, will see things differently. I have hope in you, young Stephen. That may be why I spared your life." He looked at Stephen's face. "You are not surprised. No? You too know the facts of life and war, young as you are, I see. We should have picked your brains, and then my—king would have ridden with you on his saddle for his shield to war."

"He would have been unwise," said Stephen with some sadness. "My father loves me as much as any father loves a son. I know that. We were much apart when I was small, and we have those years yet to make up. Loss makes one learn to cherish what one has, while it is there. But I tell you, if your king used me as a shield, my father would throw his sword into me as easily as he would a shield of some dead hide. I know that, but your king may not."

"Kings seem much alike, even in their blindnesses; they think hostages of more prize than they are."

They rose from the stones and took their horses by their bridles, and walked slowly out among the bracken, leading them, strangely loath to part.

"I was much moved by your face when I saw it," said the other. "I cannot explain why. Had we time to talk more, perhaps you could explain it to me. Do you know where you are now, how now to return?" Stephen indicated he did without speaking. "Kiss me then. Do not clasp wrists, son of Deira, for who knows how we may meet again or what we may then do." He himself saluted Stephen upon his forehead, and letting go his horse to use both his hands, returned his fillet to its place. "We must part now," he said soberly. "I hope we may not meet again."

His keen ears, for once, in the noise the spring made, had failed him. Too late, he heard the sound of many approaching horses. Stephen looked about in shock, and saw themselves ringed by the sound of approaching hooves.

"Our places, Prince, have changed," the other said with despair in his eyes, but a smile still on his lips. "It will be I who tastes the bitter hospitality of an unfriendly king. I knew I was a fool. So be it, to a fool."

"Run to your horse, and gallop through their ring," urged Stephen.

"It would be a useless act. I should not succeed in it; I can gage success. The world is too full of useless acts." He looked at Stephen, his eyes still kind. "Make some use of my disaster. Put your hands on my arms—so—and save yourself. Take me, I say"—as Stephen would have dropped his arm—"and keep this meeting secret, if you value your own skin. I am not brave for questioning, and they will find out what they wish soon enough. If you do not take me now, your honour and your credit will be endangered. You have said yourself you know the nature of kings, even when they are fathers. We are not mounted, Stephen, my lost hope; there is no help. They are all about us."

"It is the king himself," cried Stephen, in his turn in despair, as he recognised his father approaching.

"Play your part then, dear heart, or you are lost as well as I. I am a dangerous man to know, but you need not say so." He met Stephen's look squarely, and its questioning intent gaze. "You do not want to know my name. Believe me, it is better so."

He dropped to his knees in a position of submission, and hung his head, his hair falling over his face, cringing, the picture of a servile villein, least of the least. Stephen put his hand upon his shoulder and pushed him further down. He had asked for no help for himself, but Stephen knew he must give it. "Oh, God," he thought, "let them not see his horse, or there is no help at all." A wild, desperate plan was forming in his mind.

"Curran!" he shouted to his Welsh slave, whom he had caught sight of. "I have taken a prisoner in our woods. I found him poaching here. Hold him safe and return him to the hall for me." He pushed the stooping, cringing figure indifferently towards the man to whom he spoke. "He has no spirit, he is someone's villein who lost himself here, I think." He turned his back on his benefactor and left him and went with quick excitement towards his father. He had never lied to him, and he did not mean to lie now, but by his first equivocation he meant to tell only part of what he knew.

"I have seen the white stag, my sire," he cried, "and its doe, and she is great with young! If we make a hunt tomorrow, I will show you how to come on them."

"It is a different hunt we make tomorrow," the king said, and Stephen knew with a sinking heart his words had reached the ears of the cringing prisoner in his serf's hands. "I am in too deeply now, I shall not get out of this unscathed," he found himself thinking, "but I will yet try for what I can. Why should life be so hard as this?"

"We will hunt your stag and find its doe on our return," the king promised. "What of this man, your prisoner? Why was he here?"

"I do not know. I found him here, unarmed, unhorsed, and so I took him. He may be a herdsman or a woodcutter, or a gleaner of the forest wood. May I have him, or does your grace wish him from me?"

"I wish him," said the king, and Stephen's forlorn hope, never strong but all he could conceive, went from him. "He looks harmless"—he lifted up the drooping head and looked into the face and lowered eyes, but in the noon dusk of the forest he could see very little through the hanging hair—"but on this day and in this part of the forest, it is wise to leave nothing to chance. I will question him myself after we make a meal. You were late, Stephen, and we thought to look for you, since we had plans to ride this way this afternoon. You are well found," he said, smiling down on his son.

"I would not have given your liege cause for concern." Stephen hoped that his father could not read his face in the green shadows. They rode on, comfortably, companionably, like the good friends and the loving father and son they were, but his wits were working desperately, for he knew he had not long in which to use them. He wished it were dark, but he must use what lay to hand.

Noon dinner in the great hall, though late, passed in its usual manner. The king's minstrel played to them and sang, and it being the day before a battle, he sang of battles, and of heroism, and of one man defending a narrow pass against great odds, for the lives of his companions and his king, a theme that stirred them most in that hilly land. The queen was present, and since Stephen would ride out with his father, he sat between them. Their great hunting dogs lay beneath their feet, too well-mannered to show that they waited for the finished bones. Stephen felt the rough, wiry fur of his particular hound beneath the soft soles of his dinner shoes. He could hardly eat, thinking of the stranger who had befriended him without cause, a joke at the hands of the boys who were too young to come into the hall. He hoped that Curran could keep him from them, and would. He was wearing his richest cloak, of embroidered silk, and a jewelled fillet replaced the simple gold one he had worn in the afternoon. He looked the picture of the fair, loved prince he was, and his father smiled on him with loving favour. He himself disliked the questioning of prisoners, and he found himself prolonging the meal.

"Stephen can sing too," the king shouted. "He learned it of the monks. Fetch us your harp, Stephen, and sing to us."

It was the moment Stephen had hoped for, and though it might spell the end of his well-loved way of life, he took it without hesitation. He kissed his father's hand, and excused himself.

"I shall fetch my harp, and I shall sing for you with pleasure. Wait for me. I shall not be long. And I shall bring with me a surprise for you." He did not flush beneath his father's proud, loving gaze, but met it with his own, proud and loving in its turn.

"To pay a debt befits a king's son," he thought, "no matter what the cost. I am not ashamed for it."

The Second Division

HE DID NOT GO TO HIS ROOM. HE WENT ON QUICK FEET DOWN THE WOODEN STEPS INTO THE LOWEST ROOMS, WHERE THE PRISONERS WERE KEPT—THEY RARELY HAD THEM, AND never more than one or two at most. Prisoners were of little value to them. They kept them for ransom, or made them slaves, if they survived their first day's welcome. He found the stranger of the forest, his hands bound, sitting by Curran, in the darkest corner, away from the firelight. The young boys had found no sport with him, for Curran was a formidable guard, and now there was no one there, only the two.

"I have come to show my prisoner to the hall, since it is my first," he said, and felt Hell gaping for his soul, though he had not wholly lied. "Give me the leash, Curran."

"Will you need me to go with you, my Prince?" The idea of display was not a novel one, and Curran did not think to question it.

"He has no spirit," said Stephen, pushing him with his foot, "and I am armed, and he is not. He is not much of a prisoner after all. My first, and one that will not gnash his teeth, but still my first. Come, you!" he commanded. He half pulled, half pushed the reluctant, stumbling prisoner ahead of him, whose head was still bowed and whose whole demeanour was cowed and subdued.

Once around the corner, Stephen paused and took quick stock. He put his finger to his lips, and to the prisoner's, and formed with silent lips the words, "Trust in me." He saw the quick lift of hope in the boy's dark eyes, and he felt repaid, but his part was by no means done. Instead of turning to the right, to return up to the hall, he walked noiselessly but boldly down the long passageway that led to the small door that opened to the inner side of the stables.

"You must escape with me, not I with you," he said, cutting the other's bonds. "Take my sword, and if we meet anyone, use me as a hostage. I don't mind your stunning a groom, but please don't kill anyone, they are my friends. They are not very brave in here, you can do as you like. My horse is in the further stable, and there is an outer door there, that I know how to open, if we can only reach it."

The prisoner's demeanour had undergone a rapid change. He stood erect again, his eyes cautious but full of light, his hair tossed back. But he made no move to take the sword which Stephen held out to him.

"I will not deceive you, Stephen mine, I love you too well for it, and you are too brave an atheling. I shall tell you my name, and then you may not wish to go on with this plan."

Stephen shook his head. "Do not. I know who you are. Take my sword now, and in my house do as I say."

The other briefly bowed, in recognition, and took the sword, and with no more hesitation grasped Stephen to him in an experienced manner, and edged his way through the door. The first groom was sitting on a heap of straw, his back to the door, unsuspicioning. The former prisoner hit him expertly on the back of the neck with the flat end of the sword, but the sound brought the two other groomsmen forward.

"For the love of God, do as this man orders," cried Stephen faintly, "or he will kill me, and you too." He saw their faces whiten and their knees shake. He prayed silently that he had not misjudged the ferocity of the man who now held him in his turn helpless. The strange boy curtly ordered them to kneel down and turn their backs. He quickly dealt with them as he had with the first.

"I have not killed them, at least, I think not. I have made them sleep. Shall I leave you here?"

Stephen shook his head. "We are not away yet, and there is a long distance to pass to the spring and your horse, or through the woods, even if I give you mine. I go with you. And that will seem more natural, for you to take me. But when we reach the woods, stop. I do not know how long we have, how long my father will wait for me in the hall. I think not very long." They had mounted, the strange boy in front clinging to the mane. They did not take time to saddle the horse, but as soon as Stephen had unsecured the special fastenings, poured out through the door into the clear air and raced forward as if to catch the clear wind.

"You have left the sword!" exclaimed Stephen. "They will find it, but we cannot go back."

"I did not leave it by mistake," said the boy. "I do not want to do blood with your sword, and if swords are used at all, there will be blood drawn. Nor do you want to do blood."

They said no more in the rush of the ride. They reached the cover of the woods, and the prince requested the other to dismount. "Give me your jerkin, I see it has a hood," he said, "and take my cloak and my fillet." At the other's brief hesitation, he said impatiently, "There is not time to argue. I wore them on purpose that they might be seen and easily remarked. You must do as I say, or you will be retaken." They exchanged garments quickly, and remounted, and rode as fast as they might to the spring where the other boy's horse still waited. Stephen reined his horse in short. They did not tarry, for already the forest seemed alive with watchers.

The boy wearing Stephen's clothing touched his hand to his forehead in a gesture of respect and farewell.

"Safe journey and farewell, O Aella's son," cried Stephen, and turned his horse.

"Live well, noble Prince," responded the son of Aella, watching Stephen for one brief moment as his horse bounded with him out of sight. Then he swung into his saddle and disappeared on his fresh mount towards his miles-distant castle rock.

Stephen descended back towards the place where he should meet the hunt, if it had begun, and from the sounds he seemed to hear in the woods, he thought it had. The search would be intense because he had been taken by the prisoner, but such an escape, executed daringly in the day, would mark the prisoner for more than he had seemed to be, and they would hunt him relentlessly for himself. He waited calmly, his heart cool, until he heard a horse and then he showed himself briefly and spurred his horse in the direction away from which Aella's son had gone, to distract them in their immediate pursuit and in their later reckonings. He heard a horn blow, calling the discovery. He did not expect to escape them, for he knew their abilities, but he meant to elude them for as long and for as far as possible. If they caught a glimpse of their true quarry, the jewels gleaming in the forest light should cool any pursuit of his supposed self. His horse was tired, and he heard them closer on his heels, pacing him, but still he kept his distance, and rode on, and on, until one, more relentless in the lead, drew near, and threw his spear into his horse's hindquarter. The horse reared, and fell, but he slid from its back, his tell-tale jerkin blazoning his identity, and ran off into the shadows of the woods, where his jerkin and hood pulled over his lighter hair mingled with the shadows of the trees of the forest.

"My poor horse," he thought, the tears rising in his eyes and in his throat, "is he the first to fall? I did not mean him to. And I shall be the next, I think." His breathing was laboured and heavy, and he felt near exhaustion, but he had shaken several of his pursuers off. One pair of boots, though, came on relentlessly. He could not shake them, and he thought he knew them: Ecgfrith, who had taught him all he knew of woodscraft. If it was Ecgfrith, he had then no hope, but without hope, he ran on, and still on, sometimes pausing to catch his breath, or double back, until he doubled back almost into Ecgfrith himself. He twisted loose, and ran again, but the hunter had the close scent of his tired quarry now. In the next moment, he had run him down, had leaped upon him, even as Stephen fought and struggled like a wildcat of the woods and bit, intent on every second's delay. He heard Ecgfrith's shout, and echoing answering shouts. He felt the man on top of him draw his sword, and then he did lie still, and let him bind his arms and hands behind him. He felt his head drawn back, and the hood ripped from his hair, and then the man who held him give a startled exclamation of shock and dismay.

"My Prince!" he said, with the respect of habit in his voice, but with the common sense of a good fighting man, he did not release his grasp, but brought himself and his prisoner to his feet.

"How is my horse?" Stephen asked, not wishing to ask but because he must. From the instant of discovery Stephen had ceased all resisting. He stood now, with quiet, tired dignity.

"Your horse is hurt, I do not know how badly, or whether he can make the return to the hall."

"We have been friends, Ecgfrith, for many years. For those years, will you try to take him back, and not kill him here?"

"I would do it for the horse's sake, regardless," said Ecgfrith. "It is a good horse, as we both know, for we trained it together." His lips were set to keep the questions in he would not ask. "This does not look well done to me, my Prince, but it is not my place to ask your reasons of you. I shall take you to your father, my liege king; you may explain to him as it seems best to you."

But he made no move to untie the prince's hands, and

Stephen did not ask him to. He did not think to try to deny now what any thinking man could quickly see, for he had run from his pursuers, who were his friends. He offered no explanation, even as Ecgfrith had asked for none, and he walked quietly beside him, his head high, and then mounted with Ecgfrith's help before him on his horse. Ecgfrith did not rein in, for which Stephen was grateful, when they approached the other searchers who had converged, only shouting that he had found the prince, but not the other, and left them to continue the search, while he rode in towards the hall to meet the king.

The Third Division

THE KING WAS NOT IN HIS HALL. HE, TOO, HAD RIDDEN OUT AFTER THE PURSUIT, AND IT WAS SOME TIME, A VERY LONG TIME IT SEEMED TO STEPHEN, STANDING BY THE QUIET figure of Ecgfrith, and yet in the end too short, before he learned his son had been recovered and returned, and came back to assure himself he was unharmed. He did not wait for Stephen to approach him but strode in loving haste to him, and put his arms about him. But his son did not respond, and he noticed the unnatural rigidity of his arms then.

"Do I see your hands bound, Stephen, fastened from your use of them? How comes this?" he asked slowly, suddenly thoughtful, for his brain was like an eagle in the swiftness of its plummet.

"Why are the arms of my son bound behind him like an enemy's?" he demanded of Ecgfrith, but knowing the old fighting man's judgement, he did not ask in anger, only

45

in surprise and an incredible growing suspicion. "What have you done, Stephen?"

Stephen, grief eating at his heart, saw, as he had known he would see, that his father believed the evidence of his own eyes, without words. He felt no rancour for it. He believed in the judgement of Ecgfrith himself. And if he had hoped for one moment's doubt in his favour, and in his unexplained self, he knew the facts warranted none. His father might not see others' visions, only his own, but he had never failed yet to see facts clearly, and in their relationship and perspective of each to the other. He could see his father's mind now, as clearly as if it had been exposed to him, quickly and relentlessly and mercilessly picking out and fitting together the hitherto disjointed facts of the morning and afternoon. His face grew visibly sterner, as some sense to them emerged.

"Ask Ecgfrith," Stephen said simply. "He knows what he has seen. Let him tell you."

He watched them draw apart. He did not move. He did not wish to reveal the direction Aella's son had taken, although he hoped him well on his way home by now. He wished yet to stall for time, for Aella's son, and now, he found to his dismay, for himself, his courage wilting under that appraising stare. He felt his teeth beginning to shake, in a kind of reaction. He did not wonder that his father won his battles. He had never before been on this side of his father's face, and it struck him with foreboding, although he had expected the interview to be bad. The quiet morning in the woods now seemed impossible to explain, and he saw only that he had spoken with the son of the king with whom his father was at war, and had said nothing of it, and that he had pretended ignorance of the prisoner he took, and had to some degree successfully diverted his father's suspicions of the prisoner through his father's trust in him. He saw also, all in a second's clarity of the mind, what the presence of Aella's son, and then his emergent need of him, had blurred for him: that had he spoken his suspicions to his father—even only that it was a hostile fighting man he held—his father would not have waited for a meal to pluck his prisoner's brain. His own processes of thought his father would find inexplicable. He would only see that he had missed a confrontation he would have given much to have, through his son's conscious doing; and that Aella's clever son had penetrated his fastness and his secrets, and had lived to take the story home. Aella himself, knowing of the attack planned for the morning, might with his son's special knowledge now attack in the night.

Stephen stood there in an agony of concern. And then, like a stone into a clear pool without a ripple, the knowledge sank into his mind that the man whom he had met would say nothing to his king, nothing at all. There would be no need to, only that a prisoner taken had escaped, and he had pursued him and not found him. That would be a shame and not a treachery. But what he had learned in the saving of his life he would not reveal. Stephen did not question this knowledge that had come to him. For himself, then, he too must keep silence. That was all. However hard it might be, it could be no harder, he thought, than what he must endure if he tried to explain. What he had done had no forgivable explanation in his father's eyes, with a battle imminent. In his own eyes it had had, and it still did, but his father had not heard the voice in the forest as he had, and had not seen and did not ever see with his eyes. Their fathers must fight, as they had always intended, with no intervention from either son. He had meant no treachery, and perhaps in the end there would be none, if Aella's son kept silence too. He saw his father coming towards him, and he trembled.

"What Ecgfrith tells me is true? You took a prisoner and you let him escape you? You let him put his clothes upon you, and ran from your own men?"

"It is true," Stephen said.

"Or is it more than Ecgfrith thinks? I think myself it may be. I think that you perhaps contrived, for reasons of your own, the whole escape. Is that so? What would those reasons be?" He studied the expression on his son's face, but though he read fright, he read no answer, and Stephen himself did not speak.

"Was his capture perhaps unpleasant to you, and not what you intended? Why capture him at all? Was he of such quality that, met face to face with me, you had no other choice?" He kept his piercing gaze on his son's evasive face, piecing what he must think out of it, coming closer each moment to what he hunted in it. Stephen felt he had never known the strength of his father before, until he felt its power directed full against himself, and he wondered that he had dared, even unthinkingly, to pit himself against it. What had he expected from one who claimed descent from the great North God himself, despite his brief interim in the monks' faith? Like a great wind, his father's gathering wrath blew through his mind, and he felt he would be engulfed.

"Stephen," he heard his father's voice through the wind, "I am speaking to you, and I am asking questions that I mean for you to answer. I am waiting to hear what you have to say."

And yet Stephen also saw that the wind was held in check, for his father clearly believed that what his son would say would somehow make all clear. "Ah," thought Stephen, "if I only could." But he could not lie, and he could only hope that his father's ferreting mind would unhole a false cony to pursue. He could not reassure him, and he would not mislead him. He said, with a dignity that he was not aware of, despite the humiliation of the rope on his wrists, "I have nothing to say. You know me. I am your son. You must think what seems best to you."

More than that, he would not, and for the next hour, did not say. His father found it hard to believe his ears had heard what he knew they had. Bafflement for the moment cancelled out all anger. He sent Ecgfrith from the room, and took out his hunting knife and freed the wrists of his son. He went by the fire, and took a seat, and directed his son to come and sit by him. He noticed the wanness of his son's face, and he poured him a cup of hot honeyed mead, that had been kept waiting against the return of the fighting men who had gone out on the search, although they had not found what they thought to find. When he spoke, he spoke with all the gentleness Stephen had ever found in him.

"Stephen," he said, "I trust you for yourself, but I cannot trust you or your judgement for matters of my state or my rule or the safety of my thanes or my wife and other children or my fighting men, not to entrap them. You are very young, and I know that, and I can forgive your errors, if you will tell them to me freely, and let me make remedy for them, as I now best may. If you think I did not notice that you had taken a young boy not much older than yourself, you are mistaken. If you had a feeling of compassion for him, you were unwise, as he was unwise to come onto the land of our demesne in these unsettled times, but in that only foolish, not treacherous. His king—and who it is is what I must know and I will know from you, for I think you must know, or you would tell me you did not—his king would serve you as I would have served his man. You know that surely."

Stephen nodded his head dumbly. He had tasted the mead at his father's bidding, and the honey had flowed revivingly and quickly through his veins, but he had drunk very little.

His father's voice was urgent: "Now, Stephen, for the love there is between us, knowing I will not change in that, will you not tell me quietly, here by the fire, what I must know? You need not tell me the *why* of it, if you prefer, but only the *what*."

"Ah, but the *why* is all," Stephen thought. Though his eyes grew bright, he did not answer the king, but stared into the fire, as if he would find an answer to his own dilemmas in the leaping blue flames of the oak. His father put out his great hand and took his son's slight face in it, and turned it towards his own. His gaze, though kind still, had an inflexible purpose in it that Stephen did not mistake.

"Stephen, do not make me come the king over you, as I can and as I will, though you were my only son. Nor will I love you the less for what I do. Take care. ("Where I loved," thought Stephen, "I would take care not to tyrannise.") You know well what we have planned for morning, and morning is not twelve hours away. I cannot and I will not take your judgement on this matter, for though I do not believe any man of Aella's would be so witless as to let himself be found or so feckless, if found, to let himself be taken on my land, it was on this side of our land bordering his that you were nearest. I must sift this matter for myself. And there is Aedan to the North, and Penda's son to the South, and the Welsh have a new leader, I am told, and even the Irish are unsettled. There is no gentle herder of that boy's age, or wandering scop, who would appear so in my land, unheralded. Most men are not such fools. I shall not, if by any means I can avoid it, lead out to fight tomorrow morning before I know how great a threat comes to me from this escaped trespasser, and from which direction. Do you understand me?" He paused, to let his meaning penetrate. He thought he saw by Stephen's eyes it had.

"I do not want your opinions. I want your facts, and if you do not tell them to me *now*, with no more delaying, I will tell you what I shall think. I shall think that you know well the name and occupation of that prisoner you unwillingly took and then so willingly loosed, deceiving me, as I sat here beside your mother, with all my company of men beside me, except three witless grooms and your own slave, whom I brought back with me from Wales to give to you—and I shall break you to obtain them, as I would have broken to obtain them the man on whom you had compassion. I shall think that you have met this man not just this once, and that there is some treachery got up between you, which I shall here within this night discover from you, never think that I cannot. Is he worth the taking of his place to you? Are your secrets worth so much to you?" he asked curiously.

Stephen fixed his eyes on a rafter beam in a faroff corner of the room, and kept them there, though he dared not turn his face away, and again he made no answer, though wondering at his temerity. He heard his father sigh, and the room seemed to loom ominously before him.

"I am tired, Stephen, I have ridden long today, and you and I have far to ride tomorrow early. We need our supper and our sleep. Answer me now only these questions, Stephen, and all the rest for now I can forget. Do you know his name? Do you guess his name? Do you know the place or hall or land to which he owns? Did he give you any reason to believe he had a skill or was a fighting man? Did you speak with him before you took him, or afterwards? What did he say to you? Had he any marks upon him, any distinguishing signs or dress or build or feature that you recall, that he disposed of, or I might not have seen in my brief view? Do you know his business in my land, or do you guess at it?"

He spaced the questions slowly, leaving a pause for Stephen at the end of each, which he did not fill. When he saw his son was not answering, he addressed him once more patiently: "Are these simple questions so difficult for you, Stephen? So difficult you cannot even shake your head, or say a *no*? I wonder why they should be, and my heart misgives me at the only reason I can find. I am asking you in *this* room now for the last time. Stephen, will you answer me and tell me what I have to know?"

Stephen made no motion with his head, and he did not open his lips, but he found himself, against his conscious will, which wished desperately to protect himself, looking back straightly into his father's eyes, and keeping his eyes on his, he slowly turned his cup over and let the

hot lovely drink his father had offered him spill out to fall
sizzling on the hearth.

"I have challenged him; God help me now," he
thought to himself in savage fear, and saw his father had
not mistook his gesture. His eyes veiled themselves, as an
eagle's do, and he rose and he said in a voice that had little
expression to it, "Come with me, Stephen."

He saw his littlest brother in the upper stair, peering
at him from the arras of his mother's room, but he averted
his gaze from him and followed his father down the steps,
past the kitchen, and into the very bowels of the keep. He
knew their destination. He felt he must have known it all
the past hour, even in the afternoon, but he could not
believe it was to happen to him. He was to be made to
speak. It happened to others, to an unfortunate few, but
he had never believed he must face it himself. He wondered now why. If the unspeakable could be done to anyone at all, it could be done to oneself. He should have
known that truth, but he had not. He cast a last haunted
glance at the airy upper regions of the fortress, where the
late sunlight lingered, as his father pulled the great door
that concealed the staircase leading down to the armoury
and to the prisoners' rooms. The steps here, being below
the hall, were cut from the stone itself, instead of being
made of wood like those above, and his feet made no
sound upon them.

His father had not put his hand upon him or compelled him, and yet he had followed him as he must, and
now he waited, not trying to run, knowing as Aella's son
had the hopelessness of running from the presence of the
king. He saw his father open the door into the armoury,
and speak to the first archer, his captain, and the master

armourer. He knew them both so well. He was not only their prince, he was their friend, and they his. How would they all manage to go through with this work? How could one hurt one's friends, or be hurt by them? He supposed they would know. It was their affair to do, not his. He could not watch their faces, as the king briefly gave his orders which he could not hear, to see if shock and disbelief came over them, or if they remained as stolidly obedient and controlled as ever. He was suddenly covered with shame, and he kept his eyes fixed on his feet, as his father called him by name to come over to him.

"I shall be brave for one more moment—move, foot— and then no more," he told himself again and again, willing his unwilling feet to carry his shrinking body across the last space that separated him from the group of men. Courage was not enough in itself: it did not sustain, he discovered. Even the brief pride he saw flicker in his father's eyes at his effort did not reward him. "I have brought myself to this in more ways than one," he thought to himself in horror. "I am a fool."

The Fourth Division

HIS FATHER LEFT HIM AT THE DOOR, GIVING HIM OVER
INTO THE CHARGE OF THE TWO FIGHTING MEN WHOM HE
KNEW WELL, WHO KEPT THEIR EYES AVERTED AND DID NOT
look at him, although they put their heavy grasp upon his
slight arms in the manner they used with all enemies captured and brought to them. His father did not ask him
again to answer him or to speak, and he was glad his father
did not, for at the moment his resolution failed him.
Through the half-open door he could see the fire gleaming, in which the irons lay heating, to mend the weapons,
and to do worse things with. He saw the rack, and the
chains on the wall, and his face whitened and his heart
failed him.

"I am not going to make it," he thought to himself,
"I cannot, it is too much, O God, help me." A resolve
came to him. "I am not brave, and I cannot act it, but they
cannot make me speak. And that is all that matters."

"You will do as I have ordered you," he heard his father address the chief archer and the master armourer, "but when my son expresses he will answer for me the questions I have told him I must ask him, stop these pursuits at once and call me."

He made to go, but he saw the white piteous look of terror on his eldest son's face, and he went again to him and said, "You can stop this, Stephen. You have only to explain yourself to me in terms that I can understand."

He thought his son must not understand him, and he asked, "Do you hear me?"

"I hear you," Stephen said faintly. "I cannot."

He saw his father turn away from him abruptly. Abandoned, his legs left him and he could not walk, but the grasp of the two men held him up, and they walked him through the door. He caught a last glimpse of his father staring at him, wincing at his degradation. The great heavy door shut, and he was alone with these men, their faces not hooded, but masked more thoroughly, with no sign of recognition on their faces. He might have been the man himself, their long-time enemy, whom he had released from them. He was still not sorry for what he had done, he could not regret it, but he could not look at what lay about him, or at these former companions now implacable, their regards turned a little from him. The worst, he thought, was to be not able to look at what you did, not to cry at what was to be done to you.

He remembered suddenly in the flickering lurid light of the flames and the darkness of the upper ceiling a strange terrible vision an Irish monk, a visitor to the monastery, once told him of having. What was his name? He could not remember—he had been very old, a holy man.

He had been cast into a dark valley, he had said, where there were four fires burning, the fires of lying, and greed, and wrangling, and pitilessness, that increased and reached and joined together and burned all the world about them. But an Angel, the monk said, had lifted him above them, when he thought to be consumed in them, and the Angel had said to him, "What you did not kindle shall not burn in you." The old man had been wearing only a thin shirt, Stephen remembered, when he had told of his vision, although it was winter, and he had been covered in sweat as if it had been the hottest part of summer. His face on the left side had been hideously burned, where he said a corner of the fire had touched it in his vision, for one small sin he had made. Ah, Fursa, that was the name. He found himself sweating, like Fursa, although he was not hot.

He shut his eyes, and dangled limply in their grasp, and to his horror (and though he did not know it, to theirs), he began to cry. "Oh, God," he thought, "let me be brave, at least at first. Let me not cry." He began to think of other things, furiously, as hard as he might, of the green garth of the monastery and the little flowers on it, and the pure light within it. His lips did not stop trembling, and the tears were behind his eyes, but his whimpering noises stopped, to his relief. He knew that they removed the chain from his neck, and the fillet from his hair, and his brown tunic, and his shoes and his stockings, even the trew about his waist, until he was naked as a newt, and more helpless than the naked babes. They left nothing to protect or shield him from their will, except his mind. He fixed his attention on a monk, carefully stipling on the gold leaf onto a carefully painted sheet of vellum, in reds and blues, and he hardly felt them chain him against the wall, or lift the scourge.

His father had never whipped him. He had never had to. He, Stephen, had been gently but well trained by the monks, and he had loved his returned father so, he had needed only the voice, the touch, to tell him what to do and he had followed where his father led, as he had followed him down the steps. His fair skin was hardened and toughened, and he did not find their blows intolerable. But he knew what they could do, if they wished, and had done, and the anticipation of what might come next exhausted and terrorized him. He gasped, and writhed, and struggled to evade them, but his mind was not with them. He was watching Clausula, the oldest of them all, slowly and delicately etching the black letters, first the straight lines straight across, then the crossbars, then finally the hairline widths drawn in, slowly, painstakingly, love for his God in each stroke of the brush. Ah, he had made the error now, he had blotted the margin with a brush too full, as though he had felt the eyes of a little boy peeringly upon him. He motioned to the little boy, and showed him how he would not scratch the mark away, for there should be no errors in this work of love. "Even an error may be made an act of love," he had said, and the blot became a little dog, a little hound, entangled in a vine of leaves and flowers. "Oh God, high King of Heaven, take this mine error to an act of praise," cried Stephen silently, and he lifted up a face suddenly transfigured, oblivious of his tormentors. They stopped, aghast, and went aside to confer.

The early evening drew in, though in the lower room the light did not change, and passed slowly and yet timelessly in a fever of pain and release, and pain and again release. He shut his eyes, regardless of their commands, and would not look at what they brought to apply to him, but he could tell from the feel. They stopped frequently, and bluff and rough and hardened as they were, encouraged him to obey his father. The sweat poured from their faces, and from his, and his limbs cringed from their ministrations, and sometimes he cried shamelessly, but as the hours passed, neither were the forwarder.

He began to wonder if they would never stop, unless he spoke, and if his father meant to kill him if he did not. It did not occur to him to lie. He had never lied, and he would not know how to begin, and if he died for it, he did not want to have to go to the Hell the monks promised and spend eternity in more torments like these. He was only half conscious, but he never lost his consciousness completely. He seemed to hover, both in his unhappy body and somewhere a little way above, but not watching what was done to him. From time to time their sharp commands reached him, and he paid them brief attention. But when he learned they meant to put him on the rack, his attention came abruptly and wholly back. He had seen a man racked once, who did not speak and died, and he had seen one of his father's own men who had been racked by Aella, and had survived, and was no use now to himself or anyone, a kind of crippled, baffled monster. He had never had any courage, but he had had a sort of detachment, which now deserted him. His face was so white, and drained, it could go no whiter, but nausea suddenly overcame him, and he retched, all over himself, and the man nearest him, who cursed involuntarily. He began to cry, pitifully, and in earnest, helplessly, hopelessly. He knew they would pay no attention to him, and they did not. Their faces again averted from the stinking, sodden mess he was, fastening his trew again about his waist, they half carried, half pulled him in his unresisting, helpless form across the room and stretched it on their machine, fastening his arms and legs by the wrists and ankles to the ropes at the four corners. When it was done, he left off crying then, and he looked at them, and he said, in what voice he had left, with sudden, unexpected dignity, "Do you do this to your prince?"

"We do as we are ordered by our king," the armourer said, his eyes not looking back at Stephen, and bent to his work. As the ropes tightened, Stephen felt an agony pierce every several muscle and joint and organ of his body, all at once, like a piece of music played on all strings. He had not imagined anything so exquisite in pain to exist. He heard the armourer question him, but he did not answer. He shut his eyes so he would not see when the armourer turned the ropes, and gasped for breath, throwing back his head and vainly seeking release. As more pain shot through his nerves and his bones and his muscles, and more terror through his mind, alone and abandoned in the dark night in this cellar, he began to pray, quietly and earnestly, with all his strength, for a quick death, or for some release.

"O Jesus, sweet Christ, bound upon the rood, come to my aid," he prayed. "O Thor, piercer and thunderer, strike them!" His thoughts wandered between the conflicting heavens and divinities of his house. "I am lost, I cannot endure," he prayed silently. "What is given to those that cannot endure?"

After a time, he realised his concentration was such that he no longer felt the pull of the cords; and the flickering heat of the fire and the voices of the archers seemed to have slipped away from him. There was nothing about him at all, except empty darkness and sometimes something like soft cloud, and then, incredibly, ahead of him, somewhere, he heard laughter. He willed himself to reach it.

The Fifth Division

"MAMA," SAID MARGERY, BURSTING WITHOUT WARNING INTO HER MOTHER'S SITTING ROOM WHERE HER MOTHER SAT WRITING A LETTER, "THERE IS A BOY IN THE GRATE behind the pianoforte."

Her mother looked up, a faint frown puckering her pretty brow, under the bunch of drawn-back curls, and without putting down her pen held it carefully in arrest, and looked at her middle daughter absently: "A boy, my love?"

"A boy, Mama, and he is as real as real, but he will not speak to us, and he has the saddest face."

"You are imagining things, my little one, and I and your father have only yesterday warned you against it, and has not your father promised you a whipping for it, if you do not stop these fibbings? He does not like it, nor do I."

"Peter has seen him, too, but Alyson has not, but then, she will not look. Does that not prove to you that I

am serious, and not telling you a story? I was practising
my music, just exactly as you and Miss Marlin said to do,
but the exercises were very dull, and I thought to play the
berceuse that is new, and then Miss Marlin came in, and
made me do the exercises again, and after she had left, I
suddenly lifted up my eyes, for just a moment, and then
I saw this boy looking at me, with an amused and somehow very understanding smile in his eyes, and I thought
someway he wanted me to continue with the berceuse, but
of course I could not, for Miss Marlin was not far away,
and so I told him as much—"

"Margery," her mother answered in a firm voice that
quenched her daughter's quick-running prattle, "that will
do." She laid her pen down and looked at her quenched
but unrepentant daughter, at her mouth holding back by
firm compression her eager words that looked to be wanting to escape and any minute might. "Now, daughter,
come take me to this boy you have found, and show him
to me."

She rose carefully, her slim silk skirts rustling in the
slippery way Margery loved to listen to. She privately did
not believe that there was anything to see, but it was as well
to be sure, and it was as firm a way as any, perhaps, to
stop her daughter's storytelling. Margery had once described in detail an old man who had come to the house,
but no one else had seen him; and, even to the cakes she
ate, an elaborate tea she had had at a lady's house which
no one else could find. But this last story was far too far
beyond the line, and her mother was sorry for it, but she
was already thinking she would have to send her errant
daughter to her father.

They had descended the stairs now, slowly, that

Margery had ascended so fast, and entered the small saloon where the instrument stood, gleaming and dark, with its carved rosewood panels, and its brackets where the candles were lit in the evening. It stood near a white latticed grating, or venting, with narrow white poles, triangular, that stood under part of the stairwell, like a small enclosed room with a sloping roof, and vented on both sides to aid in ventilating the air between the small saloon, with its narrow windows opening onto the terrace, and the hall itself. There was a narrow door that opened into it from the neighbouring closet, but the children, she thought with gratitude, had never found it, and she had sometimes stored their Christmas surprises in the darker recesses there, and once some special cases of a wine she had ordered for her husband's birthday, who was so hard to please and so difficult to hide anything from, but that time she had succeeded. Her thoughts had wandered. She pulled them back to where her daughter stood, almost hopping on one foot in her eagerness.

For just a moment she wondered if it was today she was having the sweeps, and one of the boys had gotten lost, but how here she could not see. And what a mess on the white wood that would be. She remembered with a shudder the time some years ago when one of the sweep's boys had gotten lost in the high chimneys that branched and wandered through the upper regions of the house. They had sent another after him and they had found him, but they might not have. It had happened to the Colonel across the mere. It made her shiver now, just to think of it, and to remember how frightened they had been. And then the master of the sweeps had whipped the boy, but her husband had stopped him. Her eyes misted. Her husband was stern, and silent, even taciturn, but he stood between her and the world's brutalities like a rock. Thinking of which she had named her youngest son Peter.

She remembered the time he had found a tenant on one of his farms, where he experimented with the grasses that interested him most of all, taking animals in traps, in a way he had forbidden, and found the wounded animal, maimed and crying. Although the tenant had been taller than he was, and was said to be very brutal, and she knew he had a gun and her husband was not carrying his, the white, angry look on her husband's face and a note she had never before heard in his voice as he told the man to pack his things and leave within the hour had sent the man meekly, his surly talk vanished, to do as he was bid. She had never seen him so angry, except the time of the sweep. A strange, inquisitive, entirely just man, she thought, with a sweet, infrequent merriness, perhaps a little stern with his boys, and remote with his daughters as they grew out of babyhood, however much he clearly loved them. Margery surely did not get her nature from herself—could it have come from some wellspring in her husband not by herself tapped?

She remembered suddenly one afternoon when he was to meet her father formally as her suitor, and they were driving in the phaeton near the ice-covered mere, and his attention suddenly was caught by it, looking at the imprisoned rushes near the edge, and he had decided to test if it would bear the phaeton's weight. It had, fortunately, but they had stuck fast, and it was only with the most exceeding and gentle patience that he had loosened the wheel and coaxed the frightened horses off the slippery surface. They had been late, she remembered, for dinner and for their appointment, but it had not non-plussed him. A little voice reminded her of her errand: "Mama, why don't you look? I have told him you are here."

She obediently stooped slightly and peered into the faint gloom where a few rays of the hall sunlight dustily shone. She could see nothing at all. She had not expected to see anything at all, but still she was angrier than she had expected to be. Margery was only twelve. Could she already be entering adolescence? Might it take her this way?

"There is nothing there at all, Margery, and you know that very well," she said with unusual severity in her voice. Her daughter, however, was not taken aback.

She peered through in her turn, and agreed: "No, he has gone. I wonder why? And how could he have done so?" she added, in a sincerely puzzled voice.

"How indeed?" murmured her much-tried mother faintly.

"I think you do not believe me!" her daughter said fiercely and accusingly. "He was sitting there, as real as real, on the floor, his knees drawn up, and his hands around his knees. But he was not an ordinary boy," she said, wrinkling her nose as well as her brow in her effort to concentrate. "Not like Peter, or Jody, though he was more Jody's age than Peter's—I forgot, I must call him Joseph now. He wore his hair differently—it was long, not so long as mine, but to his shoulders, and it was a light brown, and there was a gold fillet, a gold band, around his forehead that kept it back, from falling in his eyes, you see."

"Perhaps he was a girl," her mother suggested with unusual irony that was lost on her serious Margery.

"No, indeed he was not, for all his long hair. His face was a boy's, and so sad and troubled, for all he liked the music, I came to you so you could help him. I thought he might be hurt, the way his face and eyes looked at me, but he did not look hurt. I could not see any. He was not wearing clothes either like Peter or Joseph. They were cut differently, and they were all brown, except for a gold chain he wore about his neck that hung down long. He wore a kind of jacket almost to his knees, and for the rest, just stockings of some kind, and some soft boots."

Her mother, truly shocked, gave her a sharp slap on the cheek. "You have been in your father's book room, although I have told you you may not go."

"I have not, truly I have not!" cried Margery, in bewilderment at this sudden unexpected and undeserved attack, for she was innocent of the charge. "I have wanted to, but since you told me I might not, I have not gone in again. Though the school-room books are so very dull."

"Where else did you get such strange ideas from unless from there—or from some picture in one of Joseph's books?"

Margery, realising her mother did not see the boy, as she herself did not now, and did not believe he had ever been there, and that it was hopeless to try to convince her further, only shook her head and her quick-running tongue lapsed into silence.

Her mother spoke decisively, though reluctantly. "You will miss your tea, Margery, and you will go to your father's study and wait for him to come in. You will

sit in the blue chair, with your back to the window, and
you will not touch his books at all, and you will wait
quietly and ponder what future happiness there can be
for little girls who tell such very big stories—I will not call
them lies, and yet I hardly see what else they really are.
Do you understand me?"

"But what of Peter?" faltered Margery. "Peter saw
him too."

"You must govern Margery, not Peter," answered
her mother, "and I am thinking your eyes see persuasively
enough for two." She ignored the large frightened eyes
of her daughter, in which a sense of injustice shone even
more clearly than her fright at waiting in her father's
forbidden study, and escorted her firmly to the door and
seated her in the chair and left her there. She closed the
door, also firmly, but she did not lock it, for she trusted
her daughter in such matters of obedience, despite the too
fertile nature of her imagination.

It seemed a very long, very weary while to Margery
before her father came in. Although she did not doubt
what her eyes had seen—and she knew very well the difference between the stories she made up, giving her
imagination free rein until she more than half believed
them herself, and this fact of vision that had befallen her
unprovisioning eyes—in the end she hardly cared, she
thought, especially since the strange boy had not seen fit
to stay. She had only fetched her mother in an instinct of
helpfulness, for generally her mother was of the greatest
help and kindness.

When finally the door opened, and her father came
in, he did not at first speak. She looked at him mutely,

wondering what he would do. She was twelve now, and if he spanked her, she thought she would die of the shame. But he did not do that. Instead, he took a ferule from a drawer in his desk, and took her shrinking hands in his and turned the palms up, and struck them sharply, not mincingly, five times on each. She bit her lips, until she could feel the taste of blood, and her eyes filled with hot tears of pain and humiliation, but she did not cry, or beg him to stop.

When he had finished, he looked at her with stern eyes and said to her with a touch of sorrow and regret in his voice, "Since you have learned to tell lies like a boy, I have punished you like a boy, but I would rather have my little lady Margery in this house. I have enough of boys, and I cannot very well do without her in particular."

His gentle words did make her cry then, but she choked the sobs back, and only the scalding tears running down her cheeks betrayed her, and the congestion suddenly in her nose so that she could hardly breathe. He gave her his handkerchief to blow her nose with, since she seemed not to have hers, and then he smiled a little at her, from some part of his face, even though his eyes and mouth did not relax their sternness.

"Now, Margery, your mother tells me you interrupted your practise. I would like you to go back to it and finish it, and then take yourself to the kitchen and they will give you your tea there tonight." He looked at her straightly. "Will you try, daughter, to curb your tongue, for my sake, and for yours, and for us all? You disturb us so."

She did not know what to say. She had not told a lie,

69

but if she said she had not, he would be so angry with her again, and she could not see whose good that would serve. So she only said sincerely, "I shall try to please you, Papa," which was a true expression of her inner heart.

She walked slowly back to the music room and the pianoforte stool. She was half fainting with the lack of her tea and the strain of waiting for her father to come and discipline her; and although the thing itself had been less than the fear of it, her palms smarted and burned and there were long red welts rising and two cuts that were slightly bleeding. She looked at them quickly and then away. She did not see how she could play with them or bend them, but she must someway do as she was bid, so she could be released from this room into the kitchen and then her own. She did not even glance at the grate, but as she stumbled through the exercises miserably, the tears of pain and self-pity dropping from her eyes, she became insensibly somehow aware of eyes penetratingly and summoningly upon her.

She ignored them, though she felt their increasing calling intensity, and she said under her breath, "I will not look at you, boy; I will not look. I have been punished enough for you. You need not call me so. I will not look at you again."

Then, to her unbelieving ears, incredibly even to her, she heard the faintest whisper of a voice say just her name, "Margery." She felt a thrill run through her, of a kind she had never felt before, and hardly aware that she had moved, she slipped off her pianoforte bench and knelt by the grate. She could see the boy's dark eyes that had been fixed on her.

"It has been done to me, too," the boy said sympathetically. "I know how it feels. But you are a girl, and your father ought not to touch you. I am sorry, Margery." As she looked at him bewildered, not speaking, he added, "Margery? Is that not your name?"

She nodded, mutely, still.

"I thought I heard them call you so. Such a pretty name, for such a pretty girl, much prettier than our names."

"My father says it makes him think of stars and daisies, but it just makes me think of spice. Why did you leave, and not let my mother see you?"

"Someone called me, and I had to go, and your mother might not have seen me anyway. She may be too old, and she may not have your kind of eyes."

"Why are you speaking to me now, when you did not before?" she asked, half puzzled, half accusing, but mainly interested to know.

He shook his head. "I don't know. I could not. Now I can. I rather think"—his dark eyes seemed to look right into her—"that it is because you have been hurt for me —because of me."

"You are not a real boy," she stated, though not positively, having absorbed his last answer without commenting on it.

"Oh, yes, I am very real. I eat, I sleep, I need water, like you, to live, I can be hurt, I like to laugh."

"Are you hungry now? I am."

"No." He shook his head. "I have had my supper elsewhere."

"Was it better than my tea will be?"

He laughed at her. "I don't know how your tea will be, so I can't say."

"I will bring you some. Shall I?"

He shook his head. "You will have enough trouble getting some for yourself. And if you brought it in here, your father and your mother would be angry all over again with you. And anyway, I don't think I can eat here."

"How did you know what my father said?"

He smiled at her almost impishly. "Ask rather why you didn't see me when your mother came."

"I do ask. How do you get out?"

"I just flew away. Something like that."

Her face expressed disbelief. She had never made up anything half so preposterous as this herself.

"You will be whipped if you tell lies," she said sternly.

"I have been whipped already, so many times, one more will not matter," he said, but with a touch of reckless gaiety.

"Where were you whipped?" she asked slowly.

"On my hands like you, and on my shoulders, almost everywhere, though not my nose. I have even had the irons put to me, but you could not imagine that."

"I mean, in what place of land, not what place of you."

"It would be too hard to tell you. Actually, not far from here, but you would not believe that, if I described to you the way it looked."

"Why not?" she asked simply. He did not answer, but he smiled at her cheerfully, and she smiled back.

"I don't think, even though you say so, somehow that

you are very real. I can't see through you, so I suppose you are not a ghost. Can I touch you?"

"I don't know. I'd rather you not try. Please don't. It would make me feel so odd if you could not, and I have a feeling you cannot."

"How can you talk, out of a throat I cannot feel? That seems very odd to me. Mama and Papa seem to think the Devil has gotten hold of me. Are you from the Devil?"

He laughed a peal of laughter, so hard it brought tears to his eyes. "My father thinks so too. He would agree. But truly I am not."

"Then how are you here?" she asked directly.

His face grew less merry and his eyes darkened and saddened. "I am very unhappy where I am. Finally I could not bear it any longer, and then, when it was too intolerable to be borne, I heard suddenly the sound of voices laughing, it was the voices of you and Peter and your sister Alyson, and I came to listen; I don't know how, but I did. I found myself here, where I could watch you, and from time to time, that's all I did. I could see you and hear you, but you could not see me. And then, why I don't know, you could. There is nothing more I would know how to tell you. May I come again?"

She nodded. "Why are you dressed in those clothes? They seem very strange to me."

He laughed. "Your clothes seem very strange to me too." Suddenly a look of anguish crossed his face, and he said, "I am called back. I must go. Have your tea. Turn around and finish your music but play the sweet one, not those dreadful noisy exercises. And don't look back at me. I will try to find the way to come again."

She did as he asked her, without questioning. When

she ventured to look around again, the grate was silent, and empty, as she had known it would be. She went very quietly, thinking, into the kitchen to have her tea, and she included the strange boy visitor, whose name she did not know, in her grace.

The Sixth Division

He HAD BEEN BROUGHT BACK SUDDENLY TO CONSCIOUS-
NESS BY A SUDDEN BURST OF WATER THROWN ROUGHLY IN
HIS FACE. HAD THEY RELENTED? NO, HIS QUICK-RETURNING
agony told him even before his brain that they had not,
that his limbs were stretched as tautly as before on their
rack. "God!" he thought, "I cannot endure this. Let me
faint again." He felt himself slipping away again, but the
icy water in his face again pulled him into his intolerable
present. He had been somewhere pleasant, where his tor-
mented brain could not remember. Someone was sobbing,
and from the state of his throat he supposed it must be
himself. Had he screamed, too? Probably. He had so little
courage for this kind of death. Had these men, these soldiers, always hated him? Did they hate his father, too, and
him, because he was his son? Or just himself? Or did it
bother them to do this to him? He had known them a third
of his life. He had played with that bluff armourer there
whose face swam before his tortured gaze, had ridden on

his shoulders, and followed him about adoringly, he who now bent to tighten ropes that were too tight already.

He heard a door open, and someone came in. Then the icy bath roused him, and he saw his father's face wavering before him. His lips parted, and before he knew it or could stop them, the words formed themselves, "Help me!," naturally, effortlessly, to his former source of all help. He saw his father shut his lips and turn away, at his cravenness, no doubt. His father would never himself have pled for help, his father himself had had him placed here. Then he had gone away and left him here, all day. In his agony, he began retching, although he had hours ago thrown up all that he had in him, except his actual organs, and he expected any moment his very heart to burst. Yet had he known it, these men had actually been very gentle with him, as far as was consonant with their orders and their duties, and they had not injured him in any permanent way as they so easily might have done. They waited now, disgust at what they had been forced to do barely concealed on their faces, for the further commands of their king. At first they did not come. The king could not bring himself to speak.

He had stayed away because he could not bear to witness what he felt his state's security demanded, but when hour after hour passed, and no word was brought to him, he could not wait in ignorance any longer. If his son died for it, his state's security suddenly seemed of less value, for though he had younger sons, this eldest son, his heir, seemed to him in large part that very security. And he did not doubt now that for reasons incomprehensible to himself his son intended to die rather than to tell him what it was his due to know. Only he would not die, except by accident; their orders did not go so far as to allow that to happen. His strange, gentle son, born of his earliest youth, so fierce in battle and yet so mild, like a woman, he thought, cursing the ill-fortune that had made him a captive to the Welsh those many years when his son was growing up: how he had found the strength to withstand what grown men so rarely could? If he had tempered his orders to the age of the subject, it was no idle play. He had not conceived his son had either the will or the power long to resist him, once force, brutal if not ruthless, was applied to him. His world seemed fallen about his ears, and for perhaps so little: some David and Jonathan friendship; and was he King Saul?

"Has he spoken of these matters yet at all?" he finally asked. "Has he said anything, any word, at all?"

The captain shook his head. "We cannot keep him here, he keeps slipping away from us."

The king did not ask for explanation. He forced himself to walk over again to his son, to his torn, bleeding skin, livid in the firelight, and his fair brown hair matted with sweat and blood. He saw the boy was conscious, but he also saw that he shut his eyes at his approach. He put his mouth close to his son's ear.

"Stephen," he said, "I cannot bear this either. I will help you but you must help me too."

"You must bear it," his son whispered, his breath barely carrying the words, "if I must. If I can, cannot you?"

The king's face looked greyer than his son's, and he said with entreaty, "will you not speak of what I must hear? Stephen, I have no choice, but you have."

He had to bend to hear his son's faint words: "It is I who have no choice, sire, but you have."

The king turned away, and said only to the captain, "Do what you have to do; he must speak and he must speak quickly," and left the room, hearing, even as he left, the screams wrenched from his son. He hoped the walls were thick enough that his wife could not hear. These castles were strange places, he thought, life going on, dinners and beds, on top of such agony, but none stranger than an island castle where he had been, with the lady's bedchamber, her chests, her tapestries, above the underwater chambers for such as this, not two feet removed above it by the stone. Did she know? His thoughts scattered in the rending sounds so near him. He leaned his own head against the wall, pressing it into the rough stone, in a lesser agony. Abruptly, there was silence, and the wooden door behind him opened, and the captain came out. His face was sweating, and his big hands were nervous, both from the scene behind him and the scene before him, but he spoke bluntly.

"I have released him."

"You have what?" the king said sharply. "Did he speak?"

The captain shook his head. "Is it your intention now to kill the prince if he does not tell you what you wish to know?"

The king shook his head slowly. "It is not."

"Then, sire, allow me to know my trade. I know the signs. He will not speak, he has gone beyond it now; but he will die, or not recover to himself, but be a helpless cripple if he does not die, if we continue with this questioning. So I released him. Sire, he is not *there*—it is no use to ply a person who is gone."

The king stood with no sign or expression on his face, but he said, "Take him then into one of these rooms and lay him down."

"I shall put him in my own room, on your permission. It locks," he added, "and we live all about it."

"Are you, or is anyone here, able to be a physician to him, or does he need more?"

"I will suffice. I have been careful, sire, because he is our prince, and we have loved him, though I daresay he does not think it now."

The king watched the captain re-enter the chamber and waited until he came out again, bearing in his arms the limp, bruised body of the king's son. He walked beside him into the small private room which in the absence of prisoners the captain shared with the chief armourer, and watched him lay the boy down on the bed. He looked so helpless and so broken and so far from dangerous that the king's heart smote him. His son's eyes briefly opened, and looked at him with an unreadable expression, and then slowly closed again. He did not open them again, though the king, covering him with his cloak, stayed beside him until he had to leave to armour himself.

The Seventh Division

PETER CAME RUNNING INTO THE BIG KITCHEN, IN HIS NIGHTGOWN AND HIS NIGHTCAP, BUT WITHOUT HIS SLIPPERS, AND FOUND HIS SISTER WITH HER FEET ON THE FENDER eating bread and jam and drinking a forbidden cup of tea beside the cook. It was past the cook's hour to leave the kitchen, but the cook was so fond of Miss Margery that the cook had stayed on to keep her company.

"Law," said the cook, "you should be in bed, Master Peter."

"It is too light to sleep," Peter said briefly. He could not hold his news. "Margery," cried Peter, "you must come quick." He leaned to her ear and in a loud whisper announced, "That boy's back."

Margery got up at once, and without relinquishing her cup or her bread, followed Peter out of the kitchen, up the stairs and down the hall and into the music room.

"Don't crumb," said Peter with an anxious glance at his sister's bread, "or we shall really be for it."

She did not deign to answer. She was peering hard inside the grate, but there was little light. "You must get your candle, Peter. I cannot see him. Is he really there?"

"He is lying on the floor," Peter said as he scampered out to get his candle. "I had my candle then, but I left it in the hall."

"Boy," said Margery softly. "Boy, are you sick? It is Margery. Can you hear me?"

"I hear you," returned the boy's voice, now well known to her. "You do not have to call me Boy. My name is Stephen and you may use it."

"I may use it? Do people where you live give permission for their names to be used?"

"Yes," he said. "But I will tell you later. Margery"— his voice was faint, and she put her ear by the grate—"what I said earlier was not true. I have not eaten supper, I have not eaten since noon, and not much then. No, it is not a custom where I live, it just happened. Will you let me try what you have in your cup, and your bread? I am so hungry I am faint."

"But the cup won't go through the grate," she said, "though I can put pieces of my bread through."

"There is a little door here," he said. "Can you imagine where it may lead?"

She screwed her brow up and thought hard. "It must be in the closet, behind the cloaks. Wait—here is Peter with the candle. We will try to come."

They were enterprising and inventive, and in a few moments they had deciphered the catch to the door and stooped and entered inside. The boy whom they were to call Stephen had sat up, and was waiting for them. Margery, not sure what he would do, placed her tea and her bread before him.

"Turn your backs," he directed them. "I am not sure what to do, and I may look very silly."

"We wouldn't mind," they reassured him, but they did turn their backs.

"I didn't know the boy could talk," whispered Peter, astonished.

"Of course he can talk," whispered Margery back. "And his name is Stephen."

"How do you know?" asked Peter suspiciously.

"Silly, he told me so, of course." Peter, speechless, had no reply. They continued speechless, the two of them, waiting for Stephen to tell them to turn back.

"It's all right," he said after a moment. "I can pick up the cup, and it doesn't fall, and I can eat and drink it. It is very good, but what kind of drink is it?"

"Why, it's just India tea," they said, "with milk and sugar."

"Milk I know," he said, "but no sugar and not tea. Which is which?"

"The tea is the brown drink, and the sugar makes it sweet but it is melted in the hot," they said in turn.

"Ah," he said, "like honey."

"Well, not very much," said Peter, "for honey is stickier and has more taste."

"Stephen, have you never drunk tea?" cried Margery in amazement.

"I never have."

"Well, I'm not supposed to either, it is very bad for one, they say; though I cannot imagine why when it makes one feel so good. Can you?"

"No," said Stephen, "I cannot imagine. I feel as if I had the strength of ten after drinking your tea."

"Then tell me," said persistent and curious Margery, "why must we have permission to use your name?"

"I have three," Stephen said. "My family name, which I am not going to tell you, but which everyone where I live knows; and my Ekename, which is an extra name, which I am not going to tell you either, though someday I might; and my real name, which I do not tell everyone, but I have told you, and you may use."

"How strange," said Margery. "I must ask Papa if he's heard of it."

She looked up suddenly, and the boy Stephen was not there. She gave a little gasp, and then she said matter-of-factly to Peter, "Hurry, we must go out of this closet. If Mama catches us, or Papa, they will do much worse to us than slap our hands."

"Look!" said Peter. "I've found the Christmas candle holders." She paid no attention to him. She picked up her cup, but as they turned their backs and bent and were going out the tiny door, they heard Stephen's voice behind them saying "Wait."

Margery was so surprised that she almost dropped the cup, but she had had the presence of mind, knowing herself, to hook her thumb through the handle. Peter was both cross and pleased.

"You make me dizzy the way you keep appearing and disappearing. I think I may lose my supper. I wish you wouldn't."

"Wouldn't what?" asked Stephen, smiling. "Wouldn't appear or wouldn't disappear, or both?"

"Wouldn't disappear, of course. Why don't you stay, I have a thousand things I want to ask you."

"I doubt if I can do that—I cannot seem to remember either place very well when I am in the other." He looked at the little girl. "Have you a thousand questions, Margery? And is there any more tea in your cup?"

"No," she said frankly, "and only five or six. But we can't stay. Alyson will be nearly through her bath, and Miss Marlin will want me to take mine, and she will be looking for me."

"Can you leave this grate?" asked Peter practically.

"I think so. I can try."

"Then follow us and we will take you to the second nursery that we don't use now, and we will bring you some more tea, and when Miss Marlin puts out our lights, we will come and see you, but you must keep this candle by you, for we are not allowed to use the tinderbox. It's a good thing I did not drop it when you gave us such a start."

They went first to the kitchen, and found a breast of pheasant, which without scruple they took, and a second cup of tea left in the pot and sugar and milk, and a fruit for their guest, but to their surprise he did not want cake.

"It is dangerous, I hear, to eat or drink in another world, for it has often meant one cannot return, but I should not mind, for I do not like mine. It is not just because I am in disgrace, I do not like it very much at any time. I am glad I can eat. I feel much better."

"Are you in disgrace?" asked Peter wide-eyed. "When I am in disgrace, I am sent to my room, and if I am naughty too, I am whipped by Papa as well. Were you sent to your room?"

"They are fiercer than that where I live, but then I am older than you, and considerably more in disgrace than you could possibly know how to be. I do not see how I shall ever come out of it. Perhaps that is why I found a way to come to see you. But as Deor says, 'This too may pass.' Only I hope your house does not pass. I like it so much here. Will you mind such a disgraceful one as I in your house? You see, I am being very frank with you."

"We do not mind. We love to have you come here. You know we do. You do not even need to ask. Why are you in disgrace?"

"It is odd," he said, "but I cannot remember."

"I shall be in disgrace for taking the pheasant," said Peter. "I hope I can forget that too. Perhaps they will think the Hound got in." He saw Stephen's eyes on him suddenly stern. "Yes, I suppose that would be dishonest."

"Well, I'm very glad you've risked it," said Stephen, the sternness crinkling into a smile. "I feel so very much better now."

Margery reached out her hand and took his quite naturally, and they neither one thought it strange. "Come, Stephen, we must hurry."

They met Miss Marlin in the hall, but they did not expect her to see Stephen, and she did not. They greeted her like well-bred children and passed demurely on.

"I am coming for my bath, Miss Marlin," Margery explained, "but I have left my doll Amanda in the old nursery where I was playing."

She hurried on down the hall, and into the nursery. "We shall not be long," she promised. "Do you think you'll stay?"

"I'll try to," he said, "though I cannot promise, for

I do not know. But I would like to. Do you know what your doll's name means?" Margery shook her head. "*She who ought to be loved.* That is a good name for your doll, Margery, I think," he said, smiling down at her. He paused and looked around. "It is a lovely room. And what a lovely bed. Our beds are hard. I should like to lie on it until you come back. Would you mind?"

They reassured him on that count, and left the candle, shading it, and scampered off. They found Alyson dawdling in her bath still, trailing her white washcloth through the murky soapy water.

"It is a swan," she said firmly, and would not move, at Margery's bidding. "Now it's going down to rest." Miss Marlin forced her to eject herself, but she fell into a heap on the floor under her towel, only the bottoms of her feet showing. "I am a slug," she proclaimed, and slug-fashion slowly humped herself into the hall.

"Oh, Alyson," exclaimed Margery in a fever of impatience. She leaned over to Peter. "She is too young, I think, let's not take her. Don't you agree?"

Peter, delighted to be thought not young, agreed. "I am going now to bed," he announced virtuously and popped himself into bed. He shared a room with Joseph, but Joseph did not have to retire himself until later. He closed his eyes and pretended to be at once asleep, and by the time Margery in her nightrobe and sack and nightcap appeared in the doorway, bearing her eiderdown, he almost was. He was wide awake again immediately. Peter was like that, she thought: no nonsense; it made him a good companion.

"I have brought my eiderdown for Stephen," she

announced. "His hand was cold and I thought he might like it."

"I'll bring him mine too," said Peter in a spirit of self-sacrifice.

"Silly," said Margery affectionately, "no one needs two, and Joseph might notice it is gone." They peeped furtively out into the hall, and seeing no one, they crept quietly down the hall and into the night nursery.

They thought at first Stephen was asleep, as Peter had nearly been, but he opened his eyes at once.

"You have been crying," said Peter tactlessly and accurately. "Why?"

"You are right," said Stephen, "but you should not say so. A gentleman—isn't that what you want to be?—if he noticed such a thing would act as if he did not."

"I don't want to be a gentleman, though Joseph does," said Peter. "I see no advantage in it. Why were you crying? You are too old, aren't you?"

"Oh, Peter," sighed Margery, "you are as young as Alyson. I wish I'd never brought you."

"I brought you," he reminded her accurately. "You did not know Stephen was back until I told you. You did not even know his name."

"I was crying," Stephen said quietly and firmly into the middle of their quarrel, "because I have been hurt today, more badly than I have ever been, and it frightened me, and I do not feel very well after it."

"When Joseph is hurt, he does not cry, and if he is frightened, he does not admit it," chastised Peter relentlessly, his new idol a little tarnished in his sight.

"I think Stephen is very brave to admit to us he was

frightened," said Margery. "I was terribly afraid of Papa this afternoon, and I am not ashamed to say so. And though I did not tell him, he knew it, and he did not mind or think the less of me. I hate pain and to be hurt, though people tell me it is good for me, but I don't believe it."

"You are very kind, Margery," said Stephen, not looking devastated by Peter's censure. "But though it is not good for us, and we do not like it, sometimes we learn things from it we would not anywhere else." He sighed. "But it is a hard school."

"I learned nothing from Papa except to keep my mouth shut, even if what I had to say was the truth," said Margery unconvinced. "That does not seem much."

"It may yet be useful," murmured Stephen with a slight smile.

"What did you learn?"

"I don't know, so perhaps you are the one, Margery, who is right. I was also crying, Peter, because this morning my father will ride out in his armour to battle, and for the first time since I could ride I will not be with him."

"In armour?" exclaimed Peter at the visions this opened up. "The horses too?"

"No, just the men. Metal is scarcer even than a good horse, and they sweat so they would rust it quickly."

"Why will you not ride with him?" asked Margery, practical as usual. "Is it because you are here? You don't need to stay for us."

"I have offended him, he is very angry with me. He will not let me ride, I think, though he has not said so; and I am not certain now that I could sit my horse."

"Do you wear armour, too?"

"I have."

"Oh," cried Peter in ecstasy. "I wish I were you. Perhaps we could trade. What kind of armour?"

"It is not so much fun as you might think," said Stephen. "It is link mail, and though you might think if you have seen it in pictures that it looks light, it is actually very heavy, and one has to wear a heavy jerkin under it to protect the skin from being rubbed away. And if it rains, or blood or sweat gets on it, it rusts right away, and then it is the very devil of a job to clean."

"Blood?" cried Margery faintly. "Have you ever killed a man yourself?"

"Many," he said briefly. "It is not very hard. The hard part is being not killed yourself, and that I am more proud of. I killed my first when I was twelve. Before that, my weapons were too small and light. But I do not enjoy it."

"What is your sword like?" asked Peter with excitement.

"It is a very good sword. It is not like an iron sword that will snap in battle, and it is not like an ill-wrought sword that will bend. It is true-tempered, by a magic process we have but I cannot explain to you. Sometimes the magic works, and the sword is worth its naming, and sometimes it does not, and then it is not worth the breaking of it. Mine was made for me on my twelfth birthday by my father's smith, who was an apprentice to Wayland. My father found him on a foray, and hamstrung his legs, and brought him home."

"*What* did he do to him?" gasped Margery.

"He cut the tendons in the back of his legs, behind his knees," said Stephen indifferently.

"How cruel!" breathed Margery.

"It is a custom," said Stephen. "I never thought about it, but it is cruel, I suppose. Though after a while it does not hurt them. All the good smiths are crippled, so that they cannot leave and go to a new master, or be easily stolen, and our smith, having his skill from Wayland, is the best living. I know many kings who would kill a hundred men to have him, without a qualm. We keep him well guarded and no one but my father knows where he stays. When I am older he will tell me—or he would have told me. I do not know now what he will do."

"I do not see what is so special," said Peter. "If your sword is flexible but does not break, that just means that it is made of steel."

"*Stele*," repeated Stephen with interest. "I do not know the word, and yet you know what I mean by it. How strange."

"My father's blade is steel, but we don't think anything about it. And if he snaps it, he just buys another, but it is expensive."

"Buy a sword?" asked Stephen. "He does not own a smith?"

"We don't own anyone," said Peter. "We have to pay the men who work for us for what they do."

"We pay the fighting men," said Stephen, "with battle spoils, but not the men who work. Some we own, from wars; the others are just glad for our protection. I would like to see your father's sword."

Peter shook his head. "I would be whipped if I touched it when he isn't there."

"Yes, I can see, you are rather young for swords. What is the name of your father's sword?"

"The name?" repeated Peter. "I don't think it has one."

"Then it must not be a very good sword. All good swords have names, like Faithful, or Ever-ready, or Friend-in-need, or Trusty, and some have more mysterious names than those. They are inscribed on the blade, and if the smith is good, sometimes burnished into the blade. Sometimes the name is on the handle, but not often. The handle sometimes breaks, but a good blade never."

"Does your sword have a name?"

"Of course!"

"What is its name?" asked Peter with great interest.

Stephen looked at him consideringly, and then he laughed, and said, "I shall not tell you."

"Oh, Stephen!"

"No, you are too young. It would make my sword angry. And anyway, I may change its name, or add to it, and call it *Stele*." He looked at Peter teasingly with his quicksilver smile, but he was also serious, and he did not tell the name.

"But you didn't tell us how you clean your armour," said Peter, his mind reverting. " 'And then the blood gets on it and it is the very devil of a job to clean,' " quoted Peter with relish. "How do you do that?"

"You take a big barrel of sand, which someone has had to find and bring in from a lake or from the sea, and you put the rusty armour and the sand together in the barrel, and then you roll it and shake it and push it and pull it until the sand scours away the rust. It doesn't take much brain, once someone discovered it would work, but it takes a great deal of time and lots of muscle."

"Have you ever done it?"

"Many times, but I prefer not to. And I would rather wear light breeches like those you had on this afternoon. What are they called?"

"We call them trousers, and they are made of nankeen material, and so is Peter's jacket. His shirt is lawn."

"Like trews?" he said questioningly to himself.

"Oh," exclaimed Peter, his eyes still shining, "I wish I could ride a horse in armour, and carry weapons that would kill, and kill many men with them!"

"You are too bloodthirsty, Peter," exclaimed Margery, horrified, "and you do not even know what you are wanting or talking about."

"Indeed he does not. It takes getting used to, all of it, the weight, the blood, the cries. The worst is when they are not killed at once. We do not have many old men where I have lived, and almost none have scars. When we are wounded, we do not as a rule recover. And almost all are wounded, one time or another. The blades, you see, are rather dirty, and we have no ways of healing, really, and we do not know much to do. But the stories the old men can tell! We cherish them."

"I *should* like it. I should not mind a little wound or even a great one, and I should recover."

"You would *not*, Peter," said Stephen. "Let me tell you what happened to my cousin. He was not very much older than you, and quite as foolish as you, and he thought he would like to see a battle. He had never seen one, for generally we make them and go off to do it, but this time one had come of itself right up to the castle wall. So he went to a window, although my father and my uncle and everyone else had expressly warned him to stay inside and quite away from windows or abrasures or apertures, but when no one was about he *would* do it, and he stuck his head out to see, and he was seen, just like that." Stephen stopped as though the rest was obvious, and there was no more to tell.

"And what happened to him?" breathed Peter.

"What do you think happens if you are seen in a battle? He was hit. But the horrible part was, and he deserved it for his curiosity but it was too bad for anyone to say so, an arrow struck him right through his right eye and so into the brain. He had had the sense to put a helmet on, but it did no good."

"And did he die?" asked Peter, the enthusiasm in his face waning.

"What do you think, Peter? Of course he did. But he was lucky, he died right off. He must have hardly felt it, after that first moment. He was dead before we reached him. But it was horrible to find him so."

"I am not so sure now I would like to live where you live," said Peter, sobered.

"I had much rather live here," said Stephen, "in your wide private warm rooms and with your wide windows that go up and down and have these transparent sheets in them and curtains to adjust the light, and walls that go right up to the ceiling. Our guest rooms don't. There is always a space left at the top, so that the host can hear if the guest plots against his life; and likewise the guest can hear the sounds of treachery. But it is more likely to be the first. A guest is sacred in a strange house, and he is never to be hurt within it. And I should like to read your books. You have so many. More than I have ever seen, and you are not kings' children. You aren't, are you?"

They shook their heads. "Our father is a baronet."
They did not ask him if he was, and he did not volunteer
to tell them. He noticed the eiderdown hanging loosely
in Margery's astonished hands, and seeing she had forgotten, he asked, "Is that for me?"

"Yes, I brought it," she said faintly. She handed it
to him and he pulled it up around him.

"How light," he exclaimed, "and warm, like the
downy feathers of a bird."

"Yes, it is an eiderdown," she said. "Don't you
know?"

"You look cold too. There is room for all of us," he
said and invited them to curl into it at the bottom. They
were all soon as warm as nursery toast.

"We only need hot milk now," said Margery wist-
fully.

"I'll go and get some," offered Peter bravely. "But I
must have the candle." He departed towards the black
regions of the kitchen, his little light twinkling bravely.

"If Joseph comes, hide under the eiderdown," directed Margery. "Can he see you?"

"I don't know," said Stephen, "it all surprises me as
much as you, what can and what cannot be done. My
limbs don't feel like mine at all, and I cannot feel the bed
beneath me, and yet I can feel this puff."

They sat hunched in the folds of the puff, at either
end, without constraint, or fear, in the darkness of the
room. They could only see the lighter darkness of the
square of the window, with the brightness of the night
sky gleaming beyond it, and one great dartling star hov-
ing, it seemed, right outside it, like a great aster.

"Stephen," said Margery after a bit, "how can you

understand me, and how can I understand you? We are speaking, we are not thinking, and you sound almost like me, only your voice is a little harsher and a little breathier, more in your throat—but you do not know what tea is, or window glass, or an eiderdown, or all kinds of things people have known about for simply years, ages even. And you know about things that happened a long, long time ago, you know them well. And so I do not understand how you can speak the way I do."

"I have the gift of tongues, Margery, and you have a sharp mind."

"The gift of tongues? What is that? And how does one get it? And can we all have it? Who gave it to you? What is the gift of tongues?"

"Ask me one question at a time, Margery, and I will answer if I can. What do you think it is?"

"I suppose you mean that you can understand and speak languages that are even not your own. Joseph is like that. He learns languages very easily at Oxford ("Oxford?" asked Stephen, but her running tongue did not pause), and when he took his Continent trip, he could easily learn to speak whatever language the country used that he was travelling through. My Uncle Oscar has it too."

"Your Uncle Oscar?" repeated Stephen, but he did not press the question. "That is a gift of tongues, but not exactly what I meant, but they may be somewhat alike, like glass and diamond. You see, I can understand the language of the birds, when I pay close attention, and the animals, even the horses in your stables, and your dogs. Not easily, but if I try, I can. Can Joseph do this?"

"You are teasing me, Stephen," Margery said doubtfully. "Of course Joseph cannot. He learned the languages he knows, and no one knows how to understand the languages of creatures."

"No, but I was given to understand them. That is why it is called a gift."

"You can understand what our Hound would say? And that nightingale I hear so faintly outside in the tree?"

"It is not so rare, Margery, there are several others I even know of besides myself who have found the way to it. But there is usually only one in any place at any time. There are not many. It is no skill, only luck, I think, and perhaps it has to do with the inquisitiveness of one's nature. I have more of that than I've found good for me."

"How did you find the way?"

"In Ireland, where I have been on an expedition, there is a pool where a great Salmon lives, and many smaller salmon, and over that pool there hangs a hazel tree, and when the hazel nuts grow ripe and fall into the pool, and if you catch a salmon that has eaten of the nut, and eat the salmon, as soon as it is caught, you will have the gift of tongues."

"How strange," murmured Margery, believing him. "How did you know to do it?"

He laughed. "Sweet practical Margery. That is indeed the point. I knew because I came upon an old man who had just caught one such of the fish. His name was very like your governess, he told me. I had my sword, and he thought I meant to kill him with it, but of course I would not have, for he was very old. And I am not a killing sort of person, unless I must. But I was hungry, and he offered to share his fish with me, when he saw me put my sword down. And I was so hungry, before I knew it, I had eaten it all. I still remember how I burned my fingers in my haste, and sucked on them, and suddenly all about me, the world grew clearer and brighter, and I saw the old man was not really old at all, and I could hear the conversation of two birds upon a tree above me, and they were speaking with excitement of what I had just unwittingly done, and then I knew."

"Were you frightened? How noisy the world must be for you."

"I was younger, and the fish was very good. I remember I was excited, mainly. I went about, hunting for things to listen to I had never heard before. I forgot about the old man, and I looked back, and he was crouching by the pool, still as a stone, or a cat, and suddenly he pounced his hands into the water and brought them out filled with another dripping, wriggling fish, which he quickly cooked and ate. He said that he came every year, at the time the nuts dropped down, for being in the magic trade, he said he had to keep his powers sharp. But he said mine would do for me, for all I needed it. But I do not hear, unless I listen carefully, you see. That is how all magic is. There is always some *catch*, something that one has to keep taking into account."

"You can do magic, then?"

"A little. Cannot you?"

"None at all. I never knew anyone who could. Do some for me!"

"Oh, Margery, how silly you can be. Magic is not so strange. It used to be the stuff by which we all lived, and not strange at all. It was needed every day. But you are surrounded by magic someone has made, and you do not see or need this older-fashioned kind of magic. Why, it could lie beneath your nose like dust, and you would only brush it away—or sneeze it away," he added teasingly. "You are used to bigger, more important things. And you have perhaps lost the key to it now."

"I cannot think of anything bigger or more important than magic. I would rather know how to do it than have windowpanes or eiderdowns. Are you a kind of witch?"

"I most certainly am not. I am a very ordinary sort of person, and now I am in a deal of trouble, and my magic could not help me at all, to help myself. It never does. It is only the most trivial kind I know, and it is of no use in helping one out of difficulties."

"You are here—"

"True, yes, that is true; but I cannot stay, I must go right back."

"Why don't you stay, if you would like to?"

"I hadn't thought of that. I must think about it some, another time."

"Stephen," said Margery pleadingly. "Do just a little magic for me. Just a tiny piece. I don't really believe you can. Show me."

"Silly little girl," he said, smiling indulgently, in the dark. "All right, I will. Where do you keep your comb?"

"On my dressing-table top, of course, Stephen."

"Well, look for it there, when you go back to your room, and—where do you keep your clothes?"

"In my wardrobe."

"Then look on the top of your wardrobe, take a chair and reach."

The door opened then, and Peter came back in, with a tray and three mugs of milk.

"I warmed them on the embers of the fire," he said,

"and the embers winked at me like eyes, and I was so afraid."

"You thought Grendel would grab you, out of a dark corner and bite your bone-casings?" Stephen said, half laughing, half scaring them.

"Who is Grendel?" they both asked in chorus.

"You don't know who Grendel is?" They shook their heads in the candle's faint light, and Peter's hand, shaking too, made the shadows jump gigantically on the wall.

" 'Then from the moorland, Grendel came stalking: he bore God's wrath!' " Stephen intoned in a voice altogether unlike his own, low, rhythmically and musically intoning. "Rather like the moorlands here. Watch out, Peter, put the candle down, you'll set the eiderdown and us on fire."

"And what happened?" cried Peter, too excited. "Tell me!"

"Oh, don't," cried Margery, "he is already afraid because of your story about the arrow, and he will never sleep. I am afraid of it too."

"But tell us a story," begged Peter, "so that I will not think of the arrow."

"Please," said Margery, "and then we will go to sleep, and you can stay here if you like."

"I do like. It is very restful here." They sat sipping their milk in silence.

"What shall I tell you?" He thought. "Something peaceful. I know, I shall tell you about Caedmon. Do you know the story of Caedmon?"

They shook their heads.

"I thought you might not, but you should know it.

It is one of the most beautiful stories in all the world, and I knew Caedmon myself. I was there when it happened, and it is quite true, though you may find it hard to believe."

"Tell us, then," they said impatiently.

"Very well. *Hwaet!*" he exclaimed suddenly, in the same rhythmical intoning, though more sharply. They jumped.

"What?" they asked.

He laughed. "That is how we always begin a story, but let it pass. This story happened in the monastery where I was staying, while my father was away, and I was placed there by my mother for safekeeping. I was so young I was not even christened. They gave me the name of Stephen there. I will tell you about it sometime, and about Abbot Stephen, though he was not the abbot there. I grew up in the monastery, but my mother was not there, although it was a divided monastery where men and women both might stay. I was just a little boy, and I was happier with the cowherds of the nearby hall, to which Caedmon belonged, and the stable brothers of the monastery than with the holier men who did the copying of the learned books inside, and I grew to know Caedmon well, only that was not the name we used to call him by. We called him by his Ekename, which was far ruder, and had to do with cows. I did not know his real name then, though others may have known it. He was tall, and very beautiful in his face, although he was not young, and strong, and he knew everything there was to know about the animals in his care, particularly the little foals and calves, and their nudging ways. I loved to be with him, and I found in him all the knowledge I desired, but nevertheless he was what you might call a—"

"— a slowtop?" put in Peter, hanging on his story.

"That is as good a way to say it as any. And he was very humble, and he knew it, he knew his limitations, and in the stables he did not mind. But it was the custom in the hall for every man to eat together, great and small alike, the thanes and the herdsmen, the clever and the learned and the unskilled who worked best with the cabbages, and all of us present, after the meal—"

He interrupted his story, his mind wandering back. "Oh, Peter, you cannot imagine such meals. They were great feasts and went on and on, and I used to steal away from the monastery and pretend I was in my father's hall, and no one seemed to notice me, by Caedmon. I was too young to be there, but they knew something of my history, and they let me stay and did not send me out. In the monastery we had very meager food, not to tempt us. One friend of mine had trouble with his flesh, and he would sometimes dream of meat pies and roast flesh, and see visions of them, and one time, but that was in another monastery before I knew him, he leaned forward in the church thinking the wooden rail before him was a meat pastry and took a great bite out of it. How his teeth must have hurt him, and the abbot whipped him for it, too, and made him lie all night before the altar on his face, saying his prayers. Our bowls, I meant to say, were very plain, unlike the carved goblets in the hall, and had ears on either side, to encourage us in humility when we picked them up in both hands and drank from them. And all the time we could not say a word. No word at all. And one of the most learned monks would read to us an edifying story while we ate.

"Would you have liked that? It was instructive, but the great hall to a little boy, you see, was more enjoyable. And there after the meal, it was the custom in that particular hall to pass the harp about, from hand to hand, round the long table, and each one as the harp came to him in turn, must take it and sing a song of praise on some high subject. Could you do that, Peter and Margery?"

"I cannot play the harp at all," said Peter and Margery.

"Well, you would have had to learn. But it was not a large harp, like your mother's, Margery. It was a small hand harp, rather like the little Irish harps. And not so difficult to play. I learned to play it, after some sort of fashion, though I dreaded seeing that harp coming closer and closer to me where I sat. And I would have liked to have said, "I cannot sing," and gone away or made the harp pass by me, but I never dared, for no one ever did but poor dumb Caedmon of the stables. I would wish I could take his turn for him, for sitting beside me, he would turn such looks of mute, helpless misery upon us, on his great lovable, beautiful, stupid face, and he would mumble, '*Ne con ic noht singan*, I cannot sing,' and then he would rise up abruptly and push his chair aside, and pass the harp to the man next to him, or to me, or drop it upon the table before him, and then he would go out among the stables, among the friendly dumb beasts who did not care whether he could sing hymns of praise or songs of glory among them or not. For his life among them, so gentle and so humble and so caring of every smallest detail of their meek existences, was like a hymn of praise.

"But one night, when he had done this, and had gone out to the stable, and lain down, weeping, like a big child, in his humiliation, he heard a voice calling him by his real name, not his Ekename, but his real name, which the voice somehow knew. I was not there, Peter and Margery, I am telling you what Caedmon told us all. The beautiful voice said very sternly, so that he dared not refuse, as he had refused the harp, and yet gently and kindly and lovingly, 'Caedmon, *sing me hwaethwugu*,' or in your language, 'sing me something.'

" 'Lord, I know nothing to sing,' Caedmon said, humbly gasping in dismay, and yet willing, and not frightened. 'It was for that I left the hall.'

" 'Sing me of the Creation, *sing me frumsceaft*,' the voice said, and Caedmon, long trained in perfect obedience, did."

Stephen's speaking voice paused, and in a clear pure voice he sang softly a few lines of a poem they could not understand:

" 'Nu we sculon herigean   heofonrices Weard,
Meotodes meahte   ond his modgeþanc,
weorc Wuldorfæder,   swa he wundra gehwæs,
ece Drihten,   or onstealde.' "

He broke off, although they wished he would continue singing. "*Principium creaturarum*," he said softly, more to himself than to them. "Then he came running and stumbling back into the hall, his face flashing now pale, now red, and asking for the harp, almost seizing it, he took it and began to sing the song he had sung for the angel. And we were all amazed, for it was the most beautiful song we had ever heard, not just for the words, which were very simple, but for the light of joy in his face, and the beauty of his pure voice that had been loosened in his throat. And after that, when he had left the hall and gone into the monastery to stay, he sang many nights. We kept his songs." He stopped and was silent.

"That was a gift of tongues, too?" asked Margery.

"It was indeed," said Stephen softly. "And I was there to hear it. Now you must run to bed, or you will be caught out. You are not afraid?"

"We shall kiss you good-night," said Peter shyly, and they did. "Will you be here in the morning?"

"I do not think so," said Stephen, "but you might look."

The Eighth Division

THAT NIGHT, MUCH LATER, AIMÉE WAS AWAKENED BY A SOUND OF SOBBING, VERY LOW, BUT AS IF SOMEONE'S HEART WAS BREAKING OVER SOME MISERY TOO GREAT TO BE BORNE. Her heart stood still at it. Then she quietly left her sleeping, snoring husband's side, and pulled her wrapper about her, and put on her slippers, and lit her candle, and went into the hall. She could still hear the sound, but she could not place it, or which child it belonged to or which room it came from. It was so soft she would not have heard it had her ears not long been trained to catch the tiniest cry from her children. She had heard their cries often before their nurse did. Had her husband been too severe with Margery? She thought Margery of sterner stuff than that, to go to pieces over a deserved scolding. Was Peter ill with stomach ache? He had a delicate stomach, and for all she could do, he would be finding things he should not eat.

She opened one door after the other, but her several children were all sleeping peacefully, even Margery after the excitement of finding her comb had invisibly exchanged its place. Still she heard the low sobbing. She decided finally that it must be coming from the disused nursery, that the children sometimes played in. Her heart in her mouth, she hesitated, a terror gripping her heart, remembering her second-born that had died in infancy. She was a brave woman, but she found she could not open the door. She went back to her bedroom, that contrary to custom she shared with her husband, and bent over the bed, gently shaking her husband awake.

"Joe," she said softly, "Joe, wake up. I need you." He gave a little start and a blowing kind of grunt, and then, like Peter, he was instantly awake.

"Joe, someone's sobbing in the old night nursery. I can hear them, but I can't make myself go in, it frightens me. It is like a ghost."

"Ghosts, Aimée? I don't believe it. Let me find my dressing gown and I'll go with you." He was tired, but she knew he would, for he was her rock, her center and her foundation. He got up heavily, and found his nightrobe and his slippers, and lit a second candle.

"Do you hear it?"

"Yes, I hear a sound, and it comes from the room you say. Are the children all in their beds—could one of them have lost itself in the old nursery?"

"They are all abed. I saw them just now. Oh, Joe, do you believe in ghosts?"

"I do not. Not in sobbing ones. Will you stay outside, or do you come with me?"

"Oh, Joe, I cannot come. Tell me what you see."

He opened the door, his nerves seemingly untouched, and walked over to the bed, and shone his candle down on the figure in the bed. He stood so, for several minutes, and then he walked back to his wife.

"Aimée, you must come and look. It is nothing to frighten you, but I do not know what to make of it. There is some young boy in the bed, and I have never seen him before in my life, although something about him looks faintly familiar to me."

His wife moved on silent, trembling feet beside him. She recognised who the boy must be at once, for Margery had described him. She saw the long, loose light brown hair, shadowing the clear brow where the fillet had slipped. She saw the faint brown of the jerkin, just showing above the corner of her Margery's eiderdown, and the glint of the gold chain.

"It is the boy Margery said she saw. She was not lying after all."

Her husband made no exclamation. He was silent, after his custom, and then he said, "What do you want me to do? Shall I wake him and tell him to go on? It is the middle of the night. Shall we leave him here till morning? He seems to do no harm, except he disturbed you."

"He is younger than our Joseph, and he looks ill," she said, her tender sympathy quickening at the boy's distress in his sleep. "I shall make him the draught of saline medicine I gave to Peter when he had such a high fever last month, that Knightly prescribed for him, and I shall give him some of my own laudanum, to help make him sleep more easily. Then tomorrow we will find out who he is, and what he wants here. You must help me give the medicine to him, though."

But he did not need to help, and fearing to alarm the strange boy, he stayed well out of the boy's view though within call. He saw his wife needed no help. Wakened from his sleep, the boy did not seem surprised to see her, and he took the medicines she gave him without demur. She put a cool cloth on his hot forehead, and stroked his hair, and pulled a chair over by him. When she seemed to try to leave, he held on to her hand, seeming to beg her to stay, although he did not speak. So she sat there, and then she changed the cloth on his forehead for another. As she bent to replace it, he raised his arms as naturally as one of her own children, and breathing only the word "Mother," put them around her neck and pulled her down close to him. She did not know what to think. He had a look of her own children, and her heart was strongly and strangely drawn to him. She knelt beside him, and did not attempt to disengage his arms until the laudanum took its effect and they slowly slipped away from her neck. Then she kissed his forehead, and reapplied the cool cloth, and pulled the eiderdown more securely about him.

She found her patient husband asleep in a chair by the door. She woke him, and with very little comment, they went wearily back to sleep, resolving to let the mystery wait until the morning. But in the morning the boy was gone, and there was no mark on the bed to show he had been there, except for the folded cloth she had placed on his forehead. They decided, despite the injustice, to not speak of what they had seen just yet to Margery, for they did not know at all what to say about it. The injustice they had done her would have to wait a little longer for its righting.

The Ninth Division

HE WAS AWAKENED BY A HEAVY HAND IMPATIENTLY AND PERSISTENTLY SHAKING HIS SORE SHOULDERS. HE CAME SLOWLY AWAKE, AS FROM A LONG WAY AWAY, AND SAW the face of the master armourer again swimming before him. For a moment, he thought he still must be in the hell of the rack, but he quickly realised he was not in great pain and his limbs were free, although they hurt and ached, as he had not known they could.

"Naow, Measter Stephen, tha mun wake up, tha'rt a good boy," the master armourer was saying over and over in various ways, continuing to shake him.

"I am awake," Stephen said, unable to assume his dignity under the rough shaking and his sleepy uncollected wits, and then it seemed too late to try. "You can stop, unless you're still trying to tear me in two pieces."

"Ay, that was a bad afternoon, Maester Stephen. But had we tried, you know, we should have done it. We were not proud to be a part of it, but what's to do, your father ordered it."

"I am not proud either, Anlaf. I was a fearful coward. I am ashamed to think of how I cried."

"Do not, lad Stephen. I should have done far worse myself than you." His soft dialect overcame the more formal language of the hall when his feelings were touched. "I canna bide those engines. Tha knows what they can do, tha'rt right to be afraid. Only a fool is not. But tha did not know that we were very careful, we didna want to hurt you."

"You did not want to *hurt* me?" Stephen started to laugh, but the memory overcame him, and he found himself crying instead.

"Tha knows right well what I mean, Measter Stephen. Had we not been thy friends, and thy father warned us, too, to be gentle, tha would not be here, able to laugh, and cry, after a day with the engines, tha would be dog's meat, na more. Tha knows that, but thy wits were gone."

"They were that," said Stephen. "They are not back yet. The more shame for me, then, if you were only playing. I think I truly cannot live with it."

"Tha need not be ashamed. Lad, we are experts with the engines, and we deceived you, and we did hurt you, you cannot go around them and not be hurt. We were sorry for it, but you can think that you be here and with your secrets still with you, and that is something no man ever did before with us. Your odd friend would not have."

His terrible day swept back over him, and he began to shiver, and he realised he was still almost wholly naked beneath the cloak. He said faintly, "My father said to make me speak. I heard him. Who then let me down?"

"Did you, lad? I'm sorry for it. He has responsibilities you do not know of, and you should have told him what he had to know, before all that began. Aella marching to meet him, and he knowing it, and no way to stop a battle he may now well lose."

"Aella marching?" asked Stephen faintly.

"Ay, lad, he got the news while you were with us. You should have spoken with him, and relieved his mind."

"I could not do it, Anlaf, and I cannot tell you now. Who let me loose, then, did my father after all?"

"He did in a way. The captain had you brought down, and then he gave your father his reasons why."

"He was a brave man then, and I am grateful to him for it. Where is my father now?"

"He has left for the wars. He stayed by you until he had to leave, to put on his armour, but you did not wake. Tha wears his cloak, and's spoiled it, too."

He took the cloak gently off Stephen's shoulder, and whistled slightly under his breath. "Roll over, lad, if tha canst, I want to see tha back."

"I cannot," said Stephen bitterly.

"Tha canst. Now help me," the old armourer said. He whistled again under his breath, with appreciation Stephen did not miss.

"Wode, lad, tha hast a tender skin. Tha'rt hurt, and bad."

"I know that," said Stephen bitterly. "You do not need to tell me."

"You may mind your tongue, my Prince. I have orders to move you to the upstairs room, so you will not be here when the fighting men return, and to bind your hands"—he saw Stephen cringe—"but I have not the stomach for it now, for I know you hardly have the feeling of them yet. I must do it, before afternoon, but it can wait for then."

"I would like to say that you are kind, Anlaf, but I cannot find it in me."

"Be angry then, lad, for it may help you and you may need it, to sustain this day."

"I am not angry without cause, and I do not have one."

"How you princes do stand upon your honour, you are all the same," muttered the old armourer. "I looked for the more sense in you."

Stephen laughed a little at that, though the movement brought the tears again to his eyes.

"There, naow, rest easy, lad. I shall rub you with this ointment that I had from my father, and he from his. It has special powers, and it cannot be made at all times of the year. And you must drink this mixture your mother has sent down, that she has made of herbs and hips. Then you sleep, like a sweet prince. And when you wake up, if you think your back will bear it—By Ash, I have a heavy hand, even at my lightest ("You have a paw like a bear, Anlaf," said Stephen aside)—I will steam the hot stones for you and make a heated bath and that will soak you back into yourself."

"How is my mother?" asked Stephen, when he could find a place to put his word in.

"She is much distressed, lad, as she might be."

"At me or for me?"

"A bit o' both, but she is tha mother, lad, you know how she must feel."

"I want her," said Stephen, the tears suddenly springing to his eyes again.

"A great, gawking lad like you, who can outfox your father's fighting men, a-wanting o' his mother? Shame, lad."

Stephen, out of weakness, began to cry softly, the tears spilling out of his hands and onto the bed blanket.

"Besides, lad, she cannot come here. You know that. It is forbidden. Otherwise I could not keep her from you. This is a man's place. But when I move you up at noon, you'll see her. There now, there now, don't greet now, the woruld is never so bad as tha thinks. Tha back will mend, and angers do not last."

"I think they do. We always are at war. Even the brief peace between Bernicia and Deira did not last."

"It will come again, lad, and I'll be out of work." He soothed him as gently as a woman. "Don't fret, lad, lie still and sleep now."

Stephen drowsing off suddenly remembered part of the night. "If my mother was not here, who was with me in the night?"

The old armourer understood what was in his mind. "It was tha father tha put thy arms about. He did not leave you, as I told you."

"Oh," said Stephen, because he did not know what else to say. "I had thought it was my mother. Did he suffer it?"

"He did not mind," said the armourer briefly.

The herb medicine of his mother, and the kind words of the armourer soothed him, and he fell asleep, until he again felt the same hand, rough even in its attempts at gentleness, shaking him awake.

"Come naow, lad, I must remove thee, it will never do for tha father to find you still below, and he will be returning some hour between now and dark."

"Why must I be removed, and why must my hands be tied again?" asked Stephen wearily. "I would rather stay as I am."

"Your father does not trust you in the armoury, wee lad that tha art, and he does not know in what fashion he will return. He wants thee awa' fro the doors, and awa' fro' he and his men."

"I have no strength for anything," said Stephen, the tears again spilling over. "It is a silly fear, and a cruel dislike"—he saw the armourer's lips compress—"but I know, I have deserved it. Do with me as you like." He buried his face in the bed and his arm.

"I should like to put thee in tha bed, Measter Stephen, and forget the night, but tha knows well no one can. It was yourself that was a silly cruel boy, to tha da and to us all. Your back will mend, tho' now tha does not think so, but tha hast cracked this keep open in a way that will not mend, not for my eyes to see. But it is no use weeping over it, Measter Stephen, we mun make the best o' it. Come now into tha hot bath and tha will see that tha feels better for it."

The old armourer was correct in his prescription. Stephen did feel better. He dressed with the armourer's help, and he ate his breakfast with his old friend, not speaking much. He cast an anguished look, that he did not realise he gave and which the old man ignored, at the armourer when he twisted his hands together behind him and knotted the wrists with a leather strap, but he did not complain, and he did not cry again. He understood the implications of his father's wishes better even than the armourer. Apart from the mistrust implied, he would be among the first to see, from a window he could not escape from with his bound hands, even had he had the strength, the returning army, in victory or in defeat, of his father, or the approaching army of a victorious Aella.

He walked with the armourer up the steps, finding them hard to manage with his cracked and strained muscles, until he reached the small highest room of the tower of the keep, where the stairs ended outside the wooden door. A large square window had been cut into the thick stone, making a ledge in it where one might sit and watch for whatever might approach over the far-reaching moors, that began soon after the hills: a herd of cattle, a flock of sheep, an army with its banners. The armourer left him, and closed the door upon him, and he heard the bolt slipped on the outside. He paced up and down restlessly, despite the aching of his body, for a few minutes, and then he leaned against the wall. The room was unfurnished and unused, except for observation. There was nothing in it, and nowhere to sit or to lie. After a length of time had passed, which he could not measure, but he did not think had been long, he heard the rough bolt being drawn back with difficulty, and he heard his mother's voice.

"Stephen," she was saying, "I cannot move the door. It is swollen with the rains. Come against it and push."

He did as she asked, and pressed his sore shoulder against the door. He had wanted her desperately earlier, but now he found he did not wish to see her. She could not comfort him now, and he had nothing to say to her. He saw his younger brothers and sisters behind her, attempting to peer in at this new view of their brother. He saw his mother attempt to shield him, and push them out, telling them to go away. Nothing, not even the agony of the night, had so brought home to him the extent to which he had fallen in his estate in the short time before the full turning of a sun, as her instinct to protect him and the excited interest on the faces of the siblings at the sight of his bound hands. He held himself erect, and stared back at them without friendliness, and at his mother with formality. He found he could not bear their pity in his present state, of neither misery nor comfort. He had nothing to say, and he hoped the visit would be short.

His mother, a proud woman herself, sensed the reasons for his withdrawal, and she did not press him, nor did she censure him. She looked at him kindly, her eyes very troubled, and she perceived the heartbreak in his face, and expected more for him. She made up her mind at that moment, though reluctantly, to speak.

"Stephen," she said. She paused and her words came falteringly. "I have something to tell you." Surprise replaced the aloofness on his face at the unusual nature of his mother at a loss for words. She turned away from him, and looked out of the window at some far point outside it, and for all her care, the words fell starkly, nakedly, colourlessly: "The woman who stands here did not bear you, Stephen. I mean, myself, I did not."

His lips grew white as if she had struck him on them. He said carefully, "I think I do not understand you. If you mean to tell me something, please tell me clearly, so I will know certainly what I am to think."

"You did understand me, Stephen."

He looked at her, his heart in his eyes. "Are you so ashamed of me? Even my father has not disowned me."

She would have put her hands on his shoulders, but he looked as if he might break, and she did not dare.

"You know I am not, Stephen. You know I love you, and that I always have, ever since your father brought you to me from Streanaeshalch where the monks had kept you for him. Do I need to tell you? Have I not proved it?"

His lips quivered. "If you love me, as you say, and if what you say is true, is this a time to tell me, if you had not before? Why need it be told at all, unless you are ashamed to claim me?"

She sat down on the floor, and made a lap of her skirt, and she invited him to come to her, and rest his head there, as he had done when he was smaller, but he shook his head, and stood upright. She sighed, but she did not stand up, and after a time, he came and sat down near her. She tried to unknot the binding on his hands but the knots were too skillfully tied for her fingers.

"Leave be," he said, "it is no matter. Who was my mother then? Where is she now? Is she living? Was she married to my father? I wish you had not told me, but since you have, for God's love, tell me something more."

"I did not say I was not your mother, Stephen. I have been that, I think, and I still am. I said only that I did not bear you."

"I understand you," he said, not smiling, "but who did bear me? That is important to me to know. Do you know?"

"Yes," she said, "I know. Your father told me. Your mother was the first queen of your father, although he was not king then, before he fell into the Welsh chief's hands."

"I am glad I am not a bastard," he said with a voice wholly touched with bitterness. She had never heard that note to it before. "She is dead, I suppose."

His queen mother shook her head. "I do not know, Stephen."

"You do not know! Then my brothers and sisters are bastards."

"Stephen, hush, do not be ugly!" she cried.

"I feel ugly. I am fifteen, and no one tells me this until you yourself come to tell me, when my hands are bound, and I cannot even hit you for it, and the door is locked, and I cannot leave you or your words. I could throw myself out of that window, though, and perhaps I shall, if you do not tell me the rest. If you are my mother, you would not torture me." He had a sudden thought, and he laughed bitterly. "No, that is not true. My father is my father, I come from his own seed—or so I suppose still, from your words—and he has tortured me. It fits. It is of one piece." He rose and walked to the window, and leaned against it, looking out, his back to her, and his whitened fingers.

"Would you hit me if you could, Stephen?" she asked.

"No," he said. "I would not. You know that. Please tell me what you want to say. I am sorry, dearest mother still, I do not feel at all like myself, and this last is too much for me. I will not stop you again."

"Your mother was a very beautiful, very strange woman, Stephen. Your father tells me you look very like her, except her hair was silvergilt, and her eyes were like your father's. She came from East Anglia, of the royal family there. She did not wish to marry your father, she wished to be a nun, in which she was much encouraged by the then Bishop of York whom she had known before the marriage was proposed. But your father and her family would not take *no*. Yet she would not be his wife, and she was not ashamed to let it so be known. Do you understand me, Stephen, what I'm trying to say?"

"I think I do. How then am I here? I hope I am not truly some monk's cub."

"No, Stephen, that was not the way your mother was, and your father knew it. He never had such thoughts. They would have been untrue; her nature was not like others' of this world, he said. But your father's was then, as it is now, and he is not a wholly patient man. When they laid her in the marriage bed and left her with him, regardless of her wishes, he did as you might think."

"You mean, he took her anyway to be his wife. And from that I came?"

"From that you came. But he never spoke of it, and did not press her again for what she clearly did not wish, and she did not ever admit even to that once. You see, Stephen, the Church will yet admit a wife to be a nun, if she has never been a wife. And he loved her, and he knew her true desire, and finally that she had meant what she said, before she married him. Because he loved her, in the end he wished to help her."

"Was I not hard to explain away?"

"Your father did know but he was taken by the Welsh on a raid that followed shortly, in retaliation for a campaign of his father's. He has not told you about that, has he, Stephen?"

"Not very much. I know it happened."

"I think perhaps you should know more about it. Would you like for me to tell you what I know?"

"I do not care."

"His memories are bitter, and he will not speak of it, Stephen, even to me. The king of Gwynned, Stephen, that was Cadwallon, once overthrew and ruled all of Northumbria, not so very long ago. He killed your father's grandfather, with my own uncle's help, and then was killed by your father's uncle, and Northumbria came back again into your family's rule. The Welsh have never had so strong a king again, and they have had a special hatred for your family since his death."

"That does not seem strange to me. Our own histories seem more strange to me. We love, we hate, we marry, and we kill, all interwoven in one piece; our enemies and our kin are sometimes the same. Go on, I'm listening. My father was captured by a Welsh king, and was gone ten years. I knew that. But why did they keep him there so long? Did they want him for a hostage against his father's wars, or for a ransom? It could not have been for vengeance, because he lived."

"They wanted both, Stephen, and in their way, perhaps all three. Your father's father could not at first complete the ransom that they asked for, or he thought that he could not. It was a very large one, and his treasury had been depleted by his wars. I think myself we find a way for what we want and what we value most. He had another son, an older son, at home with him. You never met that uncle, for though you did meet your grandfather before he died, this elder son had gone when your father finally was brought home, and no one at the court would tell what happened to him. Do you remember your grand-father?"

"Not very well, he was too ill to want to see me. Please go on. What happened to my father there. Do you know?"

"The Welsh were at that time, as they are still, a cruel race, more native to this land than we are, and they honoured then, as they do yet in certain parts, older, more savage gods than even Mercia worshipped before it came into our faith. Your father escaped them once, and made his way across their wild country, as wild and savage as their gods, into Mercia which his father had ruled when he was taken, but which he had lost since then without his son's knowing. Do you know who my parents were, Stephen?"

"I know you are a queen, and not native to North-umbria, but many queens have not been."

"I am the daughter of Penda's sister, that was Mercia himself, and of a West Saxon king. I was born in Wessex, Stephen, but my father put aside my mother, and I was returned to Mercia by my uncle, before him on his horse."

"What did Penda do? Did he kill your father for it?" Stephen's interest had quickened at the name of Penda, as all men's at that time did still.

"He made war, as you might think. My father de-cided he would rather leave his kingdom than his life, and Penda gave him those two choices, but not with words. I think he even came for a time into Northumbria to your grandfather's court, but I stayed there in Mercia."

"Penda's sister's daughter," said Stephen thoughtfully, "and yet you married with my father, knowing his father was Penda's bane?"

"It is nothing new, such alliances, Stephen. There has been bitter blood between the kings of Mercia and Deira for many years, as you know, despite their enforced armistices. Why, your father's sister was given to marry Penda's eldest son, and was made queen over the Middle Angles, whose kingdom his father had given him for a gift, but even though he came into her faith, she murdered him, her husband, after Penda's death, or so it was reported here. I suppose she thought it safe to do it, Penda dead. But Deira did not very long hold Mercia, as I told you, not even three years. It was in Mercia I met your father, when he came, hunted and he thought welcomed to that court, but Northumbria's influence was almost gone. Your father was then not much older than yourself now, Stephen, but he had had a harder life."

"You met him there. Did you marry him there?"

"No, his marriage had not been annulled then. And he was not there long. He was betrayed to Gwynned by certain nobles loyal still to Penda's hidden sons, and given back again. Stephen, I told you they were cruel. They did not use him well. I do not know what happened to him there, but I know other stories of what the Welsh have done. He was there until his father had a falling out with his older son, and then, feeling his last illness coming on him, he found that after all he could find money to complete his son's ransom and bring him home."

"You are bitter," Stephen observed.

"I think I am. On his way home, your father came for me, for he had by that time learned he had no wife. He was not the same, Stephen. He was no longer young, though it had not been that many years; his spirit had hardened, and toughened, and barked itself about, to keep out from inside himself even those he loved. But I went with him. I had loved him earlier, and I loved him still. But I meant to tell you about yourself and about your mother, not about myself."

"My father was taken, and my grandfather harried by those who took my father," Stephen said in an emotionless voice. "Tell me about my mother."

"Your mother took herself for safety to the monastery beyond the river where your father's aunt is abbess, and she stayed there until you were born. Then, when you were two years old, she left you with the monks of Streanaeshalch, where you know you were, on her way South, back to her home. I do not see how she could leave you, Stephen, I could not ever have. But then I could not have left your father either. She went south to an abbey below Mercia, I do not know where. I do not even know if she is still alive, Stephen. The marriage was annulled, while he was gone, as I told you, and he did not contest it. She did think to send him word of your birth, she was that kind, and where you had been placed. When he had married me, and brought you home, he said I was your mother, and in the dangerous confusions of the time, Stephen, no one thought to question it, for he said he met and married me while he was away, soon after the marriage was annulled." She looked at him, watching the effect of her words passing like clouds over his face, and she asked, "Had you never wondered why your father does not take the royal seat in York as his father did, but prefers to hold his castle in these wilder parts?"

"No. I did not know there was another way. It seemed natural to me: he was the king, he brought me here."

"He had unpleasant memories of York, and as king he might do as he liked, at least in this."

"I do not see yet why you have told me this—about my mother and my father," Stephen said unhappily. "Am I not to tell my father that I know?"

"I would not, Stephen. But I thought it might help you to see why he is sometimes hard and how he can both love and hate you."

"I could see that before. I wish you had not told me, but if it is true"—he saw her put her hand out to him—"yes, I do believe you, I cannot see why you should make so strange a story up just to tell me and make me more wretched than I was—I suppose I am glad to know it. I do wish to know what is true, though sometimes it seems very hard to find out. But this was easy. You have told me. I know now, and I believe you. But I wish I didn't. I shall not tell him."

His mother looked at him with compassion. "I am sorry you could not know your father's half-brother, your uncle, for you are very like him, Stephen, and he would understand you and you him, better than you do your father or your father does you."

"I love my father, and I did not know until now I had a half-uncle."

"He is older than your father, but he seems younger. Your father sent him into Ireland. I thought he might take you to see him when you went to Ireland, but they do not like one another."

"Why did he send him away? Did he love my mother?"

"I do not know they ever met. But you have given me cause to think, Stephen. It may have been." They looked at each other, each with the same surmise in their eyes, his mother half-frightened, Stephen defiant.

"Will you now be giving me too a father whom I have never seen?"

"You have no cause to think it, Stephen," she said slowly.

"What is my—my uncle's name?"

"His name is Aldfrith, Stephen."

"And he has lived in Ireland? What does he do? He is my father's half-brother? Why only half?"

"His mother was not married to your father's father. She was a different race—Irish, I think. Or perhaps British, for your grandfather and your great-uncle together fought Cadwallon and killed him, and they were in that country."

"Ah," said Stephen slowly, "again the Irish. That may in part indeed explain me, this person who is me. What does he do—this Aldfrith?"

"He is a scholar, and a friend of Abbot Aldhelm. He is in Hy now."

"I should like to meet him," said Stephen. "I don't suppose I shall." He looked at her thoughtfully and she answered his unspoken thought.

"Sons have resembled other members of their family before, and nothing has been thought of it. It is just that until now I never saw so strongly the resemblance that I see now, as I see it now."

"And you are shocked by what you are thinking," said Stephen, "and you cannot help yourself." He turned from her. "I wish you would go away now and leave me." He turned his head briefly towards her and gave her an odd little smile meant for reassurance, and then he turned his head back to the window, though his eyes saw nothing.

He did not watch her go, but he heard the door shut and the bolt replaced. He had not hoped she would forget. Even if she had, he would not have made use of it. He had nowhere to go, and no one to go to. In all his wide land there was no place he could escape his father for long, and he did not wish to. He did not think again of his half-uncle in Hy, for that did not bear thinking on. It was an island to the North, north even of Ireland, that was all he knew. It was so far away, and he did not have a ship. He did not even wish to go, had he leave and means. His heart lay here, in these walls, where he was, or soon should be again within them.

He found himself suddenly and desperately remembering and wishing to see Margery and Peter again, but he was in his right mind now, and he did not know the way, or how to leave himself, much as he would have liked to. He rested his face against the window which the sun had left, but he found the stone still warm from it. With difficulty he managed to lift himself onto the ledge, without falling out. The distance down seemed vast, from his height, first to the base of the tower, and then to the base of the hill where the plains began. He folded his knees into the window, bracing himself with his feet against one side of the window, and his back against the other, the warm stone warming its soreness. He stayed on the inside edge, leaving a foot of ledge between himself and the drop. He looked out again, as far as the sweep of his eye could take him, but he saw no movement at all, only a hawk, circling, watching something. Idly, his eye followed its slow, sweeping circles. He had once seen a band of hawks travelling, high and low in the air. He had counted ninety. This was a gold hawk, he thought, but it might only be the westering gold sun falling on its wing tops. He was so high, the hawk was below him, with its smooth chiselled pattern on its back. He wondered what the hawk was watching, and without moving his position, his eye became the hawk's eye, and he drifted with its intentness.

The transition, following the wish, was made without his knowledge. He found himself beneath the hawk's eye, standing on the moor, and near him, not watching him, were Peter and Margery with their ponies, just setting off across the moor. They were delighted, but not astonished to see him.

The Tenth Division

"STEPHEN," THEY SAID, TAKING HIS HANDS IN THEIRS, ONE ON A SIDE, "WE WANT TO SHOW YOU SOMETHING. BUT IT IS OUTSIDE THE HOUSE, ON A HILL. WE MUST RIDE TO IT."

"All right," he said, "but I have not very long to stay. What lovely shaggy beasts." He stroked a blowing nose. "I know they bite, but she will not bite me, I think." He swung himself up behind Peter. The pony did not feel his weight, but it clearly did not like what it sensed on its back. Stephen leaned forward a little, and gentled the pony with his hand. "Peter," he said, "if you will move forward, I will show you what riding can be like. Can you keep up, Margery?" She nodded, but they had been, and returned, and made circles about her, before she had reached their halfway. They cantered on happily, Peter in ecstasy, as Stephen showed him the steps a horse must learn in battle, the little pony following willingly as best it could.

They reached the hill, and took the small path that

led up its side, first barren and heathed, leading into ferns and small woods, and finally into a real wood of rocks and streams and tall trees rising above the undergrowth. They climbed in silence, the children in suppressed excitement, panting in their haste, until the path gave out, and then they pulled themselves up the rocks among the trees, clinging to the grasses for support, until suddenly they came out on the crest of the hill, on its far side, where the ruins of a square golden tower stood. About their feet lay the low remains of the foundation walls of the larger part of the building, the squares of the former divisions into rooms still visible, but the inner parts piled with white dirt and rock, and trees growing within and without. A flock of long-haired sheep browsed in and out of it, running ahead of them as they approached but not really frightened and not going far from them.

"It is my home," Stephen said quietly, "I am there now." He looked up at the tower room with its wide-ledged empty window commanding the far plain, where he knew he sat, and he looked at its base for the stairs leading down into the underground room where he had been, but they ended, after a step, in dirt, and there was no sign of what lay underneath.

"We thought it might be," said Margery. "And so we brought you here to see." She was disturbed by the effect it had on him, for her imagination, wild though it was, was too young to encompass the emotions he was feeling. He sat down on a stone, in the midst of the rubble, and put his head in his hands.

"Oh God, what year is this?" he asked half to himself.

"It is 1822," Margery answered. "Oh, Stephen," she said, "we did not mean to distress you."

"Oh God," he said again, in low-voiced anguish. "A thousand years are in thy sight . . ."

"Stephen," Margery cried, "don't weep!"

He looked at her with a faint smile, but he could not comfort her, or reassure her, for he could not comfort himself. He must surely have known, he thought, that in time such an end must come, but he had never thought to see it himself, and in this long past forgotten fashion. He wondered when the walls had fallen, and how, and why, and how the tower still stood. It was more compact, perhaps it was stronger, or more useful to someone. He must find the histories in Sir Joseph's book room, they might tell him. He pulled himself to his feet, glancing once again at the window where he sat, in lonely pain, watching. He could almost see the intense gaze of his own face, and far away on the plain, in the distance, the dust of approaching horses.

"Stephen," said Peter in disgust, "you are just like a watering pot. I have never seen anyone cry as much as you do, and you do not even seem ashamed. You make me feel wet!"

Stephen's tears changed to tears of laughter, but when he could finally speak, he spoke seriously, and he used the past tense without noticing he did: "We laughed easily, Peter, and we wept easily, and we fought easily, and we were not ashamed for it. We may have had the more cause for each than you. We died quickly, though we may not have died easily. We may have loved quickly, but we loved hard, we did not love easily, and our memories were long, longer than our lives. But there are times for each. There have been times when I have wished I had not wept, and have been ashamed, but you have not been there.

There should be the foundations of a large hearth in that northeast corner. Why don't you see if you can find it?"

When they turned around, from their exploration, he was not there, at least they could not see him. They were alone, and yet they were not. It was an odd feeling, and they felt oppressed, for they had no conception of what lay around them, or where he was, and he had not told them. They gave a half-startled look around them, and stood listening for their ponies, and then possessed of a common impulse, instinctively, they began to climb back down the hill as quickly as they might manage the descent. The hawk above them continued undisturbed its indolent gliding circles.

"Who is riding with the children?" Sir Joseph asked, coming into the house. "A groom? I saw them far away, out on the moor, riding towards the hills."

"There is no one here but us," his wife answered, "unless—oh, Joe—can it be that boy?"

"I could not see them well; I will see if the grooms are here."

"He frightens me, Joseph; I wish you would go after them. He is not a ghost—I held him in my arms, and his face is sweet, but we know nothing at all about him."

"I think he will not hurt them, Aimée. But we can speak to them about him, or to him himself, if we can find him. It may stop his visits. But I myself find I do not want to admit to them that I can see the boy. Do you?"

When he went to meet them, he found them returning across the moor, two children on two ponies, and no one else, and he did not speak of it.

The Eleventh Division

STEPHEN WATCHED THE DUST, STRAINING HIS EYES TO READ ITS MEANING, AS IT DREW NEARER AND YET NEARER, SO SLOWLY, IT SEEMED TO HIM, AND GRADUALLY HE COULD see his father's colours, and the mass resolved itself into individual helms and spears on horses. But even when the company of men reached the base of the hill, he could not distinguish one from another, and it was not until the troop had reached the keep's base that he could distinguish his father's figure. He thought he saw him briefly raise his face and look with his eagle's eyes towards the window where he sat. It seemed to him, in sudden horror, that the company looked smaller, and he noticed on certain horses bundles wrapped in cloaks. "I have killed them, I myself, as surely as though I had taken my own sword in hand: I shall never be forgiven," he thought, and yet irrationally, he still hoped to be.

He slipped down from the ledge of the window, and leaned against it waiting, half eager, half afraid. He found suddenly that he was very thirsty, but he had been trained to ignore thirst since he could walk. He was not comfortable standing, but yet he stood, for he did not want his father to find him any way but upon his feet. The minutes lengthened, and still his father did not come. The eagerness and the fear both passed, but he still stood, waiting, patient.

Far below him he could hear distant noises, the clang of iron, the whinnying of horses, the bark of dogs, the sound of doors, of rough steps, of men's voices talking, but where he was, there was no sound. The little of the afternoon that was left was slipping away into the long twilight that would linger for hours. The stones of the window ledge grew cold in the evening wind that was picking up. He did not feel the stones, but he felt the wind. He did not move, but he began to shiver. He heard a footstep on the stair, ascending, and his shivering increased, until he thought he must fall. The door opened without effort, and he saw his father enter the room.

His father did not speak. He stared at his son, silently, consideringly, taking in all there was to see in his glance. Stephen, in his turn, forced his eyes to lift and to return his gaze. His father had removed his armour, but he had not bathed. The sweat, the dust, clung to his hair and beard, his hands were brown with caked blood that had slipped under his gauntlets. He looked old, older than he was, and very tired. His weary eyes were dark with held-in fury.

Stephen realised his father was waiting for him to speak, but in the light of those eyes he could think of nothing to say. He shut his eyes, and pulled himself away from the wall, and stood swaying slightly. He felt suddenly a great pain against the side of his face. His eyes flew open, and he saw his father draw back his arm again, and he felt then the back of his father's hand hit him again flatly across the mouth and the side of his other cheek. He tasted the saltiness of blood against his tongue, but he made no sign or outcry, his eyes open but not looking at his father or at anything, waiting for what should come next.

"You are still silent, Stephen? You had cause to be; I know it now," he heard his father say. There was nothing he could say now. He stood, waiting, the hot blood risen in his cheeks, trying not to sway on his feet. He had not long to wait. His father addressed him, with a mingling of grief and fury in his voice whose like he had never heard before, to anyone, least of all himself:

"It was Aella's son himself. Aella's son, and we held him, with bonds on his hands, swordless, helpless, here in our very camp and castle. We could have won his kingdom from Aella, I think, with his son here. And you had to let him go. Why, Stephen, why would you do it?"

He approached his son closely, and took his face in his blood-caked hands and stared into it as though he would find the answer written on it, as perhaps he did, for in baffled anger and contempt he let it drop, as though throwing it aside. His voice rose again in biting rage and grief:

"And Osric your cousin is dead, and Oswald his uncle. They had us from the start. In some way they knew it all. Had I known this, or dreamed it, I would not have had them gentle, I would have broken you, and felt some grief for it, but not much. Oh, God, my gentle Oswald, and fierce Osric, and a good score of my good archers:

Aethric, Athemon, Torthere the Red, Aedgar, Wulfstane, Eadweard, Eadmunde, Raedhere, Othere, Aelfere, Wulmaer, Eadric, a goodly company of men, well-chosen all, seasoned, good, hardened wood, dead logs now, hacked, all of them.

"And I myself—" He stopped, his face mottled crimson and white like his son's, but with shame. "And I had killed Aella, with my own sword, or hit him near to death, and that boy of his looked at me with his axe raised, so that he might have hit me while I was recovering my sword, and smiled at me and lowered it, and took my sword and sheathed it in my belt. There was no one about us who dared move. It was like the center of a storm, when the trees stand still, and for a moment the wind does not blow. He asked me where you were, why you did not ride. I told him. And he told me—what you would not. He gave me this to give you." His father reached into his shirt above his belt and took out a bundled wad of stained material which he threw at Stephen's feet. It unfolded, and the fillet rolled out, shining dully, and the Irish cloak Stephen had lent Aella's son for his escape. "He told me to tell you this, holding my sword: 'Tell him,' he said, 'that I myself said nothing. Tell the prince that.' So I have told you, Stephen, but I do not myself believe it. Then he walked away, while his dying father, and his men, and all my own watched. I could have died for shame. Was it for this you did not die when the sun darkened and the Yellow Pest, *ille amabilis hospes*, ravaged and seized my friends here while I was away? I had thought it was another kind of luck, but I was mistaken: it passed you by because it could not reach me and left you yourself to be my bane instead. You have made a fool of me, Stephen, monk's cub with monk's blood, it would seem, instead of mine, and I cannot keep you here with me."

He sat down, and shook his great head to and fro, in an ecstasy of grief, and then he raised his head up and called to his son: "Stephen, come here."

The boy stumbled forward, his eyes blinded with tears, his hands still tied behind his back, and would have fallen onto one knee, but his father clasped him to him in his arms, and rocked him to and fro in his bear's grasp, his tears falling without shame on his son's head. "Oh, God," his father muttered, "my heart, my hope, my great joy, and now my greatest grief, to have you for my son, and you must go from me, I cannot keep you with me now." He abruptly released his son, who fell on his knees before him.

"Where must I go—my dearest liege and sire?" Stephen made his lips ask with as much firmness as they could find.

"Aedan presses me from the North, to join with Aella's son, Aella himself now; and Penda's son presses me from the South, demanding hostages to keep the peace. I had thought to send Osric, but he has escaped that fate into another. You will go as hostage in his place."

The shock in his son's stricken face moved him again to tears, but his face remained sternly fixed. "They will value so rare and unexpected a sweet hostage more than they need," he said, "and they will never dream that I will attack them with you there, as I most surely will in my good time, when I have routed Aedan and this Aella. You may tell them so, treachery's cub, for they will not believe you."

Stephen did not argue or protest. He had lost the right to argue, he had given it away with his own hand. But he knew that his father's decision was for him the end of everything. At that moment he would more willingly have given his neck to his father's sword, but he only said, "I shall not tell them. I shall do as you require me, and I accept my fate, but it is hard, my sire."

"If it is hard today, why was it not hard yesterday, when it was not then too late?" He looked at his son straightly. "How did you know that it was Aella's son we had? What hold did he have over you?"

"I did not know that it was he himself until I had released him. And then he told me, and stood waiting, for me to act. And I did nothing. I could not then. I had to let him go on as I had meant, though I knew what it meant for me. I did not tell you, for I thought you would have killed me, sire—I had not the courage—and then I would not tell you, for you hurt me so."

"I do not believe you, Stephen," his father said quietly. "These words do not sound like yourself, or what Aella's son himself told me. Do not lie to me now, we have not time for it."

"They are the truth, sire. I do not lie to you. But they are not all the truth. I did know him, but he did not ever tell me who he was. I guessed it, from the way he bore himself and from the way he spoke. And I trusted him—he had befriended me, and saved me from a cruel death. I could not let you have him broken in your dungeon, as I knew you would. He had no other hold on me but that."

"You trusted Aella's son—a wolf's cub without honour?"

"I think you are severe, my liege, but let it pass."

"Do not call me now *my liege*, again, ever, Stephen. You are not my liege son nor I your liege lord. Our ways part now. You have chosen where your free loyalty lay. Perhaps I should send you there, but I shall send you on to Mercia, and get some use of you."

"He has returned the favour. He would only kill me now, he would not spare me. I am your son, and you have killed his father." He bowed his head. "Do with me what is most of use to you now. I am content."

His father turned him around and attempted to untie his hands with his own shaking fingers, but in the end he took his knife and cut them. His son let them hang, ignoring the fiery pains of the returning circulation, but his effort was not lost on his father. He put his hands on Stephen's shoulders, and said, "You will eat with me tonight as my son. We will speak no more of this, and give rumour no more reason to use her tongue. That is my reason, to keep your usefulness as my hostage; but for myself, it is to have you this one more night as we have used to be together. For after this, I think I shall not see you again in this life on live."

That evening Stephen did not wish to remember or live through again. His father took him down again to his part of the house, and his slave brought water for them both to bathe in. He looked at his father's body and its scars, memorizing every line, and his father regarded him with the same emotion. They dressed themselves in light fine tunics, with their gold chains, and pinned their cloaks with their jewelled brooches. His father set again upon his hair the fillet of a prince, tenderly, his hands shaking slightly. He sat down and asked Stephen to comb his hair

out for him. They did not speak. There was nothing more
to say. The companionship of these last hours was enough.

He sat as before, between his mother and his father,
for in the morning he would ride out with his father, and
a small group of the fighting men. Outwardly, it seemed
no different from other such meals, but the proud light
in his father's eyes was gone, and his mother held his hand
in hers beneath the table. He knew that everyone in the
hall knew what had passed, and what had happened to
him, and where he was going, and why, but it was not
spoken of, nor referred to by any word or gesture or by
so much as an unseemly glance. It was a sad meal in itself,
devoted in its songs and speeches to the honouring and
the remembering of the slain kinsmen and friends of battle. His father took his own chain and his son's and dis-
tributed the links among the kin who yet survived. "It is
wergild I pay," Stephen thought, pierced, "I have slain
them. I should be put from this life for it, but instead I am
put from this hall, and I pay the wergild. And I eat and
drink this food I do not want, among their friends, to show
it was not I that did it. But we all do know it. Oh, God,
forgive me, was one worth so many?"

His father read his thoughts in his face. "Do not take
this so to heart, Stephen," he said. "If it had not been now,
it would have been another time. It is our lot to die in
battle; we expect it, and we do. You know that. My father
died of illness, but he would rather have died in battle, I
think, his honour and his glory newly won, intact. I
should myself. I ask only God grant me a good death without shame. These men knew no shame. Their names will
live, and they will be praised."

"As mine will not," Stephen thought. His father's

words, meant kindly, to comfort, did not. The guilt he felt for the empty seats remained. And if this was all his father wished for him, a death without shame, it was not enough, his spirit, suddenly rebellious, cried out. It was not enough.

Beneath his feet, he felt the rough fur of his hound. When the evening finally ended, and the men rose and began to withdraw, he knelt down beside the animal he had raised. He took his ears, in his fingers, and pulled them slightly, and looked into the dog's sad eyes.

"O Arctur," he cried, "will you miss me, will you whine for me where you have used to find me, or will you take another master and forget me?" He buried his face in the dog's rough fur, and clasped his arms around his great neck and wept as if his heart would break, but silently, though his shoulders shook. When he lifted his head, his eyes were dry. He gave a last pull to the big dog's ears, and a last look about the hall, and then he followed his father up to his sleeping quarters.

"You will sleep by me tonight, Stephen," his father said, "between your mother and myself." Stephen understood the precaution, which he found the kindest of any his father might make, and the affection that prompted it. He lay awake between those two dear familiar bodies, long after they and all the house were asleep, except for the watch he heard making its rounds in the still night. He did not wish to sleep, to waste the last hours in his own place in that manner, but he was very tired.

He fell asleep, and in his dreams, he restlessly relived the events of the last day, until he felt his mother's hand soothing him, and his father's heavy arm put around him. He fell asleep then, more deeply, but in his sleep he felt an overmastering compulsion to pay a last visit to Margery and tell her that he must leave, and say good-bye. A long ray of moonlight fell through the upper window onto the floor, and moved slowly onto the bed. It looked as thick and strong, he thought in his dream, as the ray of sunlight that held up Aldhelm's cloak. He thought that if he wished to, he could walk straight up it like a path. He tried, and found he could.

The Twelfth Division

He found the house, in which he suddenly discovered himself, standing awake, in deep sleep. He was
standing on a stair in a square of moonlight which
fell on him from a window in the stairwell. He walked
silently up the stairs and down the hall to Margery's room.
The door was ajar, so that she might see the night light in
the hall. He walked in, and sat down on the edge of her
bed and wondered how to wake her, and if he should. He
need not have wondered. The slight, infinitesimal weight
he made on the bed, and the fact of his presence, woke
her at once. She smiled up at him, unsurprised, sleepily delighted to see him.

"Oh, Stephen," she said, "you have come so late. Is
there a reason?"

He nodded, not trusting himself to speak right then.

"Shall I fetch Peter?"

"If you like."

She skipped out of bed, fully awake, and he walked

about her room, looking at the unusual objects in it. He touched her pen, and her bottle of ink, with particular interest, and he had sat down to try them, when she returned. He rose again, without embarrassment, when she came in again with Peter, rubbing his eyes. They all three sat down on the window seat, in the moonlight spilling into the room, looking out onto the huddled shapes of the garden plants and the shadows they cast.

"You would make good monks, Peter and Margery, to wake so easily in the middle of the night. It did not use to be so easy to wake me in the dark for Matins and for Lauds."

"Did you wake us to tell us about monks?" asked Peter in surprise. Stephen shook his head, but he did not speak, and he kept his eyes fixed on a point in the garden.

"Look!" exclaimed Margery. "There is a ring around the moon!"

"And no stars in it," added Peter in discovery.

"It will rain tomorrow then," said Stephen absently. He found himself putting off the moment of speaking, but as the silence lengthened, he realised they were looking at him expectantly.

"I have come to say *good-bye*, Margery and Peter," Stephen said.

"Good-bye?" they cried in surprise.

"I have to leave my home, and these moors, and I do not know exactly where I am going, but it will be some way away from here, and I do not think I can find my way back."

"If you could find your way here," declared Peter, "I should think you could find your way anywhere."

"Perhaps, but somehow I don't think so. It was just a

lucky chance, finding you here at all, and in my experience luck does not last. Anyway, I am not chancing it. So I have come to say farewell." He looked at them soberly, and tenderly, with feelings he did not ever have for his own so different and so differently raised brothers and sisters. "Fare you most exceedingly well, little sister of my soul, and little brother, too."

"Stephen, Stephen," they cried in distress, "you must not go yet, you have just come!"

"And you never told us the story of Grendel who came stalking, and you promised you would. You promised, Stephen," Peter repeated, knowing by some instinct the word would move him.

"Why, so I did," he said, faintly surprised, faintly smiling. "Then I must keep my promise, and I will. It is a good night for it."

"Stephen, why must you go?" asked Margery, in concern.

"I would rather not tell you," he said. She took the rebuff in silence, and he added, "My father says I must. Don't you do as your father tells you, and go as he instructs you?" She nodded. "And so do I, except just for once only."

"Which way are you going, Stephen, to the North or to the South?" asked practical Margery.

He thought. "South, but I do not know whether to the southeast, or to the southwest in that kingdom. Why do you ask, Margery?"

"Because, you see, I have just remembered that we are leaving too, on our vacation. We are going to Windemere, and then near Crewe, to see an Aunt, not far south from the lake itself. The name may not be the same for

you, but it is a long silver lake, the biggest of the meres;
it is circled by mountains, low flat hills. Perhaps you may
be going near it, Stephen, and then you could come to
see us there."

"Perhaps," said Stephen. "It does not lie in my hands
to promise, but who knows what even the next hour
holds." She did not look satisfied. He took her hand and
crossed it solemnly with his own. "Be assured, little Margery, sweet little wide-eyed, serious girl, and funny Peter,
I will come if I can. Now and always. Is that enough for
you? Shall we have the story now?"

They settled down comfortably, tucking their dressing gowns around their feet.

"*Hwaet!*" they both said solemnly. He was both
taken aback and pleased.

"Very well," he said smiling, "that is taken care of."
He held his hands up, in the manner of the storyteller,
engaging their attention:

"Imagine, a great moorland like this one, grey-green,
with the white and grey-green mists, swirling and rising,
and out of it imagine a Hound of Hell, a Hell-fiend, a
black misshapen monster, comes stalking hungrily, to the
high, horn-roofed hall where the warriors sleep. Imagine
him bursting the door, with no effort of his great hands,
and seizing like one of your dolls, Margery, a rag doll, a
great warrior in all his strength, like a toy, tossing him and
breaking him, and then cracking him and gnawing him
as I did that pheasant bone last night.

"Imagine this happening, night after night, and all
waiting, even the bravest, in fear that such a terrible fate
should be theirs, and the cowards pushing away from the
places near the door.

"Imagine the Tarnwulf, the great warrior hero, himself born of the bear in the thunder and the lightning, with a power within him as great as Grendel's—he the slow boy late to make his mark but now at last in his full strength. Imagine him catching the great beast by his arm, and not letting it go, though Grendel strains and pulls, until the hall of Heorut is ready to burst its seams. But the well-built hall holds, and it is Grendel's arm and hand which tear loose, and remain in the Tarnwulf's hands. His eyes riven now with fear, he plunges across the moor, through the mists, until he comes to the great tarn, the deep well, down whose depths he plunges.

"Imagine the Tarnwulf, his eyes as keen and flashing far darker brightness, pursuing, seeing the monster plunge, and plunging after him, into those green depths which lighten and become mixed with the light of a fire. Imagine the water thinning, in an inner cave, and Tarnwulf coming on the Hagwife, Grendel's Dam, twice as large, a great sow, and thrice as fierce a fighter. But it is the Tarnwulf who makes the blood flow from her that rises slowly to the mere top where his friends anxiously wait, and where they lose hope—not the Merewife who makes the Tarnwulf bleed, though she has wounded him with her terrible teeth and claws. He sees the magic sword, hanging from the ceiling of the cave. He grasps it, he strikes, and she is hideously dead, like her son—the sword like ice melts in her blood. But the Tarnwulf is hurt himself, despite his ringmail fashioned by that Wayland I told you of, and he makes his way, faint and gasping, up the long tunnel of the green water, to the surface, looking in vain for friends to aid him from the pool. But they have despaired of him and left, and he must pull himself out, his strength leaving him, never again to fully regain it as he had it. That is the magic, you see, Margery. Nothing is gained without something a little lost, no magic done without a loss of strength. No curse is cancelled without some echoing curse assigned. The Tarnwulf, in his way a monster like the monsters he destroyed, but now the king of the Ganes.

"Imagine then the peaceful years, the fruitful reign, the well-loved king, until the King of Hell once more sends his adversary, Fafnir, the Dragon. Imagine the fire-drake, earth-worm and night-flyer, curled upon his treasure in his cliff-lair on the headland, his great flashing eyes no brighter nor more piercing in their gleam than the Tarnwulf's. The Tarnwulf need not go, he is old now, and his strength not as in his youth. But he is impelled to go. His adversary calls him to the match. Eye engages eye, the coils of the fire monster stir. The fight is terrible, the on-lookers at their distance cannot see the way of it in the light of the fiery smoke-filled fumes. Swords, scales, jewelled treasure, breath and eyes, flash through the fire-mist. But in the end, the mighty Fafnir lies expiring, and with him, also dying, the mightiest Tarnwulf, preserving his fane but having lost himself even as he won."

Stephen's voice broke off. "That is enough. I am tired, and you are frightened. I should not have told it. Little sillies, it is just a story. Here, I shall give you the kiss of peace, and you go scampering back to bed. I shall take Peter myself, and show him no Merewife waits in the hall, and then I shall return and say good-night again to Margery."

"Do not say *good-bye*, Stephen," she murmured sleepily, when he had come back.

"*Good-bye* means *God be with you*," he said. "That

is a good thing in any case to say. I wish you would say *good-bye* to me."

"Good-bye, then, Stephen, but come back soon," she said, more sleepily still. He stood watching her for a moment, as her eyes closed, and then hesitating, he went down the steps and opened the door into her father's book room. But what happened there, although it happened at this time, will be told at another time, for Stephen put it from his mind, and Margery did not know it. In the morning, she found a piece of paper on her desk, with three words written on it that she could not read. She put them away to keep, and to ask Stephen about when she next saw him.

The Thirteenth Division

It was raining in the morning when they set out. THE TREES HELD THEIR HEAVY GREEN LEAVES TOGETHER, AND THE ONLY POINTS OF LIGHT WERE THE TINY GOLDEN TIPS fringing and shielding the new growth of the spruce. They rode in a small band, their faces sheltered and their emotions hidden under the grey hoods of their cloaks. The only sounds were the muffled hooves of the horses, the splashing noises they made in the puddles and slipping on the wet stones they picked their way through, and an occasional voice of a wet bird. Stephen did not turn his head to look back. He had looked once, long, at his home, his horse standing before the door, not his own horse that had been hurt, but a new horse, strange to him. He did not need now to look back. He knew it too well to need to look with his eyes. It rose within the eyes of his mind before him, blocking the path, blocking any thought of the new, strange place to which he was going. They did not speak, and they did not sing. They travelled down the road of the hill and a little way across the moor and then they turned South. The hills were left behind, swathed by the mist even before they were out of true sight, and the countryside rolled about them monotonously, the low land swelling in its fresh green, the heathers not yet in bloom. Stephen began to feel ill, he supposed he was catching a cold. "It wants only this," he thought, "a sneezing hostage. Thor, protect me from the last shame of a red nose!"

At noon they stopped to eat and to rest themselves near a branch of the river Tees, formerly the old border between the two provinces, Deira and Bernicia. Stephen sat some way apart from the other men, underneath a small flowering ash, where his father joined him. The snow of tiny petals, past their prime, drifted down on them as they lay at ease. "There is too much to say, and to ask," thought Stephen, "and it is for the last time. How can one live five years with a person, and love them, and when the time comes to an end, find one knows nothing at all about them? I do not even know my father's age." Instead of asking anything he could hold to, to remember, he found himself asking, with trembling lips, the question foremost now in his mind.

"What will Penda's son do with me as a hostage in his hands? Will he question me again? Will he imprison me?" The thought of being questioned again put his mind into a terror. To be imprisoned was no light matter, for their cells were not made for comfort, only for security and inconspicuousness. He could not meet his father's regard, ashamed of his fears.

"Neither, I think. He is an honourable and a fair foe, and you come as a freely given hostage, as we have arranged. You will be part of his household, I should think, although you may find you will have duties to perform you are not accustomed to doing yourself. I shall send gold rings with you, a full chain, as a gift against the expense of keeping you, and then he may use you according to your rank. You know very little and you are hardly dangerous. To question you or to immure you could only injure you or shorten your life, and lessen your value to him as a hostage. But if he should do either, Stephen, you must endure it. I cannot control what he chooses to do once you pass out of my hands into his."

"Penda's son will welcome me, as the son of Oswiu's son, I think," said Stephen whitely.

"You mean, because of Penda?" asked his father in some surprise. "There have been many deaths to lie between us on both sides. It was a just requiting. And my father had earlier given adequate wergild for ten kings, although against his will. Penda himself killed our kings in battle, as you well know, Stephen, and let my uncle on my mother's side be murdered at his court, under his own protection, against his given oath. I never understood that last, how it came about."

"Did you yourself know Penda?" asked Stephen in strange surmise, his aching head forgotten.

"I was myself given by my father as hostage to Penda himself, in exchange for Penda's daughter, when I was some years younger than yourself."

"I did not know that," said Stephen.

"It was for no fault of my own. It was perforce, for Penda then to all effect controlled Deira too, and my father had retired into Bernicia, whose throne he also claimed through his father's kin, as I do now."

"I did not know that," Stephen said again. "You never told me."

"I do not enjoy speaking of having been a hostage. It was a great shame to me, and yet, I found it interesting." He stopped, as if remembering back, and then he looked at his son, reflectively.

"You would have minded more than I did, Monk's Cub. They worshipped Odin then, and very properly, I think, being sprung, like us, from him. But I did not care, and for that matter, Penda himself, having grown older by that time, did not care either. In another man, we both respected courage, that was all. I thought him a great king."

"And your father killed him. Did you care?"

"My father killed him, as he would have killed my father, had my father not then been the better man, as Penda was when he killed my grandfather Edwin with Cadwallon's help, and with his own hand the first Oswald, both my uncle through my father, and my mother's cousin. If Penda was a great king, they were both great kings too. Does it confuse you? It should not. You have heard our history many times. And you know how Penda was killed. He had a great force, and was overlord of Mercia and Deira both, and my father had only a small force and he was ill-supplied.

"They say he prayed," he said, smiling at Stephen. "You would believe that, would you not, little Monk's Cub? As for myself, I do not know. A man's fate is decided for him, but his brain and his right arm may do much, I think, to affect that decision (whatever it may be). My own cousin, older than I, led Penda to where my father was, although they say he did not fight with Penda against my father. For myself, I see no difference in the act, nor did my father. It was on a river, the river Winwaed, not far from where we are now. It was swollen with spring spate, as this river is now, and those the sword did not reach, the waters did. The river, choked with a new debris, flowed red instead of brown. I was not there, being held at Penda's court. My own father told me of it, when he rode in to fetch me out before the news could travel or Penda's friends could kill me for it, before they fled with his sons. But these things do not interest you, Stephen, I think," his father said.

"I have never said that," said Stephen. "I cannot help it where I was raised, as you could not help it for yourself, and I would fight at your side."

"I wonder, Monk's Cub," said his father softly. "That daughter of Oswiu, still in her cradle, whom Oswiu pledged to your—to our—God if he would deliver him from Penda, she that is your aunt, was with your own abbess, Stephen, at Streanaeshalch with you. Do I see your eye kindle, Stephen, and your interest rise?"

"I do not know which nun she was," Stephen said.

"Your great-grandfather's bones, and those of my father now—it is your family too—rest in the church there."

"I did not know," Stephen said again. "No one told me."

"Your grandmother—my mother, my father's wife—lives there under their protection, but she does not even know me now, her son. It is a grief to me, perhaps that's why I never spoke of it to you. I wonder, Stephen," his father said again, "if you would fight at my side, if a question rose in your mind about what I did? Your loyalty is divided in two parts, and half is to no king who holds here."

"Do you hate me for that?" asked Stephen, not denying it.

"No, Stephen, I do not hate you for it, but it makes you of no use to me. And I send you to Penda's son, knowing very well how you will hate it. Do you find that cruel in me? Perhaps it is. You must go your way, Stephen, and I will go mine." Stephen's father spoke with a note in his voice that Stephen felt as sharply as he had felt his father's blow across his face. His father stood up, and left him, and they broke camp and continued their ride.

They rode for many hours into the night, for the light did not finally fade until only a few hours before it would burst forth again. As long as there was light to see, they rode. They slept on the wet ground, in the brief dark of that night, in their cloaks, and the next morning pushed their way to the rendezvous. Stephen did not speak with his father again, for they were always riding, or not alone. By the time they reached it, at noon, the country was changing, and in the far-off Southwest, hills were rising again, some days' journey off. They stopped by the banks of the river Humber, which marked Mercia's boundary from Northumbria. Stephen by this time had developed a fever, but he was resolved not to let anyone know of it. Penda's nephew had come for the hostage, not Penda's son himself, and their camp was visible on the far side of the river. The two groups walked their horses beside the river, swollen with the night's rains, until they reached a ford that seemed passable.

"You must ride this ford alone," his father said. He took the sword from his son's belt, and put it in his own.

"I shall keep this for you," he said, and then in a low voice that only Stephen could hear, he added, "May the road be long that brings you to my house again, or you and I remeet!" He leaned over, and kissed his son on either cheek, formally, but then he started in surprise, and his concern reappeared. "Are you ill, Stephen?"

"It is nothing," Stephen answered, his spirit withered under his father's parting curse. "I am quite well. I can ride the ford."

His father looked at him narrowly. "If you are swept away because you cannot sit your horse after all, I shall have this journey to do all over with another hostage, and another man lost. I shall lead you to the middle."

He took Stephen's bridle in his hand and signalled to his group of fighting men to wait for him on the bank, and to cover him with their arrows. Then he led his horse and Stephen's into the rushing water. Stephen felt the pull of it, and he would have been happy to have been taken by the current and dissolved in it, despite the icy spray spattering his cloak and his hot face. The hand on his bridle was firm, and the exchange made. Penda's nephew had brought a cousin to the king, a man of some thirty years, powerful, clearly a valued fighting man.

"My son," Stephen's king said briefly. "Treat him well. You may have the horse."

"Penda's son is honoured," the other said, his eyes widening slightly in conscious questioning surprise.

He was given no more explanation. Stephen turned his face a last time towards his father, asking nothing, his love and grief broadcast across it. Emotion flickered in the king's eyes and died. He raised his hand in a brief arrested gesture of farewell, and turned, and plunged without another backwards glance back across the river to where his men waited. Stephen's eyes followed him as he went, but he did not turn. A long sigh, almost a moan, escaped him, as he caught his breath that he had been holding without knowing it. The backs of all his friends were to him now, and already they were growing smaller. For the second time in a few days he could not believe that the thing happening to him actually was going to take place. He felt a tug upon his bridle, and his horse was led on across the river. His hands hung limply by his side, and he swayed.

The man beside him gasped, and snapped, "Hold your horse, Prince, or you will be in the flood!"

Stephen gazed at him blankly, dulled by illness and loss. He felt a wet stinging slap across his face, and he briefly woke to where he was and caught the saddle head and the reins.

"You are ill," said Penda's nephew suspiciously, when they had reached the farther bank, and he had leisure to survey his chilled, shivering acquisition. "Are you sickly? Is that why your father sent you?"

Stephen's face had been turned away, his eyes fixed on the little group growing rapidly smaller. Tears filled his eyes and blinded him, and he found it of no use to look any more.

"I am not sickly," said Stephen bitterly, his swollen throat hardly letting him speak.

"Then you are afraid," said Penda's nephew contemptuously. "We have a long journey before us, and you cannot ride like this."

"I am neither sick nor afraid," said Stephen, more

fiercely than he meant, endeavouring to hold his countenance, "and you will find I can sit my horse."

Penda's nephew looked at him curiously, but with
more respect. Neither said anything more during the long
afternoon's ride, but when they camped for the night, in
the shadows of the low foothills, and the evening meal had
been caught and cooked, he held out the liver and the
heart to Stephen on a stick, the red blood still streaming,
and bade him eat both that and a pungent-smelling root he
carried.

"I do not want this, or anything at all," Stephen
demurred, his stomach revolting.

"Eat them, and hold your tongue. I want no sick
babies with me. What is your name, Prince? Which son
are you?"

"I am the Monk's Cub," Stephen said, more bitterly
yet, but he ate part of the organs given him, and the biting
root that burned his mouth, and he drank the mixture of
sour vinegar and sweet mead that Penda's nephew heated
for him. "He is no more cruel than Aella's son," he
thought to himself, and he accepted the offer of the warm,
dry blanket Penda's nephew offered him in exchange for
his wet cloak, and a place by the fire on a new laid bed
of bracken. "And yet," he thought, "he would kill me,
they both would, if it suited him or his purpose, and think
nothing of it."

"You are kind," he said, with chattering teeth. Penda's
nephew handed him a warm rock to place between them,
and placed hot rocks at his feet, and around him, and put
another blanket around him, and one under his head.
"And very skilled," he added, through the warm rock,

watching him heat several rocks very hot. He placed them near Stephen's face and poured boiling water on them that steamed and hissed.

"It is my business to the king to bring you home alive, and to myself with the least possible trouble to myself," Penda's nephew said briefly, but he smiled at the wan, unhappy face of his hostage in the firelight. "Do not thank me. If I take care now, I expect less trouble tomorrow. You were sick, you see. If you are not sickly, it was the leaving that undid you. You are over young for this kind of trick," he added, "and I do not understand why your father sent you. It was unnecessary, but my cousin will be pleased. Can you breathe more easily?" He poured more water on fresh hot stones. "My father had the gift of healing, and he taught me certain skills. I find them useful, especially with a sick cub on a journey." He felt Stephen's forehead with satisfaction. "You are wondering why I came, instead of my cousin. I am a sister's son, and in Mercia that is an important thing to be. So you will be properly escorted, in a style you need not be ashamed of." He looked at Stephen consideringly. "If you are the Monk's Cub, you are Deira's eldest son. I have heard of you. No man sends his eldest son as a hostage, if he can help himself, unless there is something wrong. What is it?"

Stephen stared at the steaming stones. "My father honoured your cousin. If you are not satisfied, send me back."

"I shall certainly not do that. My brother has already gone over the Humber with your father. And I know, I think, a good thing when I see one. Were you willing to come?"

"I was willing. My father wished it." He sighed involuntarily, and he did not think he could bear to listen anymore, or talk from his throat, though he felt easier now. He saw the leather strap Penda's nephew had picked up, and he shuddered. "Please do not tie my hands," he said, trying not to beg. "I have nowhere to go, and my father has sent me. I am not going to try to leave you, I have come into your hands on my honour. I am ill, as you say, and I want to go to sleep."

Penda's nephew looked at him carefully, and then he laughed and said, "I believe you, Monk's Cub," and threw the strap down. He made himself a bed near Stephen, on the outer ring of men, not next the fire, and rolled himself into his cloak and fell into sleep.

Stephen listened to his heavy even breathing. Last night he had slept by his father, if he was his father, and last night but one by his father and his mother, who was not his mother, and heard their breathing. How strange time was, in its changes. He was there, and now he was not. He was here, and shortly he would not be. He saw the great stars shining down upon him, and he pulled the blanket over his head to shield himself from the dews that would soon fall. He was not happy, and he felt weak, and still a little ill, though his sickness seemed to be lifting, but he could bear his unhappiness. He had no desire to try to reach Margery or Peter. He had said good-bye to them, as he had said good-bye to all that was dear to him. Once before he had left all he had known, but then the world had opened, when his father returned, not closed. They, Peter and Margery, in time, and his father, in space and feeling, both seemed as immensely removed from him as they were. He was alone, with the friendly blankets and warm stones, with the cold, shining, somehow friendly, peering stars, and with the sleeping Penda's nephew a hand's reach from him. It was with these facts now he had to deal. They wanted of him only his presence, and that they had. The rest at the moment seemed of no importance even to himself.

The Fourteenth Division

STEPHEN WOKE THE NEXT MORNING WITH A CLEARER HEAD, AND THOUGH HE HAD A BAD COLD, HE NO LONGER FELT AS THOUGH HE WERE GOING TO DIE WITH IT. HE SAT UP AND looked about him. He was the last to wake. The heaps of bracken had been cleared away, and except for the embers of the fire beside him and his bed, there was no trace of the camp. Penda's nephew walked over to him, and gave him more of the hot soured mead, and the bitter root, and the last of the organ meat.

"We must ride, Prince," he said briskly. "Can you, or shall I pack you?"

"I can ride," Stephen said briefly, eating what he was bid to, with distaste. "I am well." Penda's nephew's face expressed some disbelief and considerable admiration. "You are an unusual physician," Stephen added sincerely.

"Walk then," said Penda's nephew, "to the spring there and test your legs, while I disperse the fire and this bracken." He had almost finished before he finished speaking.

The remainder of the journey passed simply. Stephen caused no extra trouble or concern to those he rode with. He spoke little, even when he had the chance, when they halted. His mind was not on past events, or on very much of anything at all. He watched with interest the unfolding of the new terrain about them and watched for signs of animals and birds and plants native to it. On the third day, they reached the castle of Penda, on a hill, much like his father's, except that it was bigger, on a flatter hill, with a tall retaining wall, and a round central keep. Just so his father had seen it once, he thought, and with just such a destination. But the thought did not comfort him, or make him feel less alone.

He was taken at once to the high hall where Penda's son sat. Penda's nephew mounted the dais and took his place at Penda's son's feet. Stephen stood there before them, a slight figure, strangely unafraid now that the worst had befallen him. The courage that surrounded him, and his frank air, impressed Penda's son pleasantly, and after a surprised greeting and welcoming, he accepted the gift of gold rings and sent him to be escorted by Penda's nephew to his quarters in the castle.

"You know who I am?" he said menacingly, when Stephen made no proper obeisance.

"You are the Battlewolf," Stephen had answered with casual indifference, not caring what befell him, "and I am the Monk's Cub."

Penda's son, surprised, had suddenly burst into hearty laughter, and when he returned to himself, he said, still chuckling, "By God, it is a brave cub. My father would have enjoyed you." He looked at Stephen sharply. "I am told we are related. Do you think, Monk's Cub, that you are my father's sister's sister's son?"

"I know that I am not," Stephen said directly.

"It is well," said Penda's son, "for I also know that we are not. Pass in peace, Monk's Cub, I shall not trouble you today."

"You may share a room with me," said Penda's nephew, "or be with the son of Penda's son, or in a cramped space by yourself."

"Choose for me," Stephen said. His voice smiled, though his face did not.

"Then I choose for you to share with me," said Penda's nephew. "I have grown used to your company, Monk's Cub. You will be questioned by Penda's son in a few days, after you have become accustomed to us and our ways, but if you answer him as you did today, you will have nothing to fear. He is not a cruel man, if his suspicions are not aroused."

Stephen found himself liking Penda's son, to his surprise, though he wondered why he should be surprised, for his father had named him both fair and honourable. His liking, showing in his face, reached Penda's son, and he responded back to it. The questioning was uneventful, unpainful, and if unfruitful of any unexpected news, Penda's son had expected little more. He was not particularly concerned with Aella's son: his interest lay with the whole realm of Northumbria, which he considered essentially one; and with the threats of Aedan to the North, and the rumours of Northmen invaders further North yet. Stephen agreed with Penda's son that it was wise to fear them, but he had no course of action to suggest that would have been acceptable to either king, and he did not propose one.

"You would do well," he said, "to make peace with my father and the two of you to make yourselves very strong, but I do not think he will accept your peace, although I am not in his confidence, and would you accept his?"

Penda's son shook his head slowly and looked consideringly at his young royal hostage. He showed him thereafter every courtesy, and gave him large access in the castle, including the acquaintanceship of his wife, and his daughters Edith and Mathilda.

Stephen gave no more thought to Margery and to Peter, but they did to him. They missed him very much, no less as the weeks passed and he surprised them with no visits, particularly Margery.

"Let us play war," cried Peter, one morning, when they were out on a hilly meadow, not far from a lake. It was a beautiful morning. It had rained in the night, and the birds had wakened late, and now their earliest songs were trilling at a time when the children could hear them. They fell on the children's ears with a clarity of loveliness that almost pained them. The mountains had emerged with the late sun, and the white mists were rising off of them. They were covered from top to foot with enormous luxuriant clumps of dandelions that held up their heads as huge as little plates, out of the milky haze, for the sun to fill them. Peter, unmoved, jumped on a little hill, regardless of the dew globes he shattered, that stained his shoes. "Let us make a battle. I shall be Deira, and you must be Bernicia."

"I do not want to play war very much," said Margery, "but if I do, it is Deira I must be, and you can be Bernicia, or I will not play at all. I *am* Deira."

"I wonder why we never see Stephen anymore," asked Peter of himself. "It has been weeks now. Has he forgotten us, or doesn't like to come?"

"Perhaps he cannot come," said Margery. "Show me how you want to play," she said, shaking the subject off.

"Well, you must be in your castle, over there, and I shall come and storm it, and I shall take you prisoner and bear you back to mine. Let me find a sword." He searched along the ground, and in a little covert.

"Stephen is not in his castle now," Margery said, remembering. "He has gone away, somewhere, he said. So you may play at being Deira if you like. I do not care which I am, if Stephen is not home."

"I am Bernicia, I have made my mind up to it. Have you a sword? Take this. On guard, Deira, here I come!"

He made a wild leap, but Deira did not stand ground before his onrush, but fled in fright.

"How like a girl," exclaimed Peter in disgust. "You will never learn to fence. Come back and hold your ground!"

"I do not want to learn to fence," Deira spoke from behind the safety of a bush, but she came slowly out and took her place again.

"Ho!" shouted Peter, waving his sword loudly at his unbelligerent enemy. They were stopped by a laugh and a voice that they knew well, and they both turned quickly around towards the direction from which it came.

"You have it all wrong, you know," said Stephen's voice quietly. He was sitting on a little hillock, not far from them. "It is not like that at all."

"Isn't it?" asked Peter, surprised. "I made sure it was. How is it like, then?"

"We sing first, otherwise it is just a butchery. Though I myself think to fight is butchery, with or without the songs. But I am a monk's cub. Here, I will show you how." He stood up on the hillock, and took a stance, and threw his head back with a wild look in his eyes, and sang in a rhythmical, beating voice, not at all like the songs they knew:

> Behold, there will be many slain
> But not I!
> Fight, fight for your friends and against your foes!
> The last one to fight is the first one to die.
>
> The earrings are flecked with blood,
> Win them before they tarnish!
> Fight, fight for your friends and against your foes!
> The last one to fight is the first one to die.
>
> If you die, we'll heap upon you
> Shields of ninety and gold hair.
> Fight, fight for your friends and against your foes!
> The last one to fight is the first one to die.

"There! What do you think of that?" he asked, sitting down again with his usual face, and his usual smile.

"I think it is very fierce," said Margery, "even for a monk's cub."

Peter, astonished, recovered his voice. "I should not like to meet you in a battle, I think," he said weakly.

"But you like to play at it," Stephen said severely. "People, even children, become in time what they play. That is why we play. Margery plays with her poppet-doll, as if it were a baby, or sometimes a grown lady, and in

time she will have one and be one. That is her vision."
His eyes rested on her, thoughtfully. "What is your
vision, Peter? Is it to be a warrior, and die a warrior's
death? It is not mine."

He had picked up, not noticing, a small round stone
from the ground, and had been rolling it between his
fingers. He looked at it with surprise. "I have found a
thunderstone! Here"—he tossed it to Margery—"it will
keep you from spots and protect your house, and all your
children." His voice did not sound as if he believed it
would.

"What is your vision, Stephen?" she asked, holding
the stone in her hand.

His eyes grew quiet, and he stared a long way off.
"I do not know. To have caused so much trouble, and I
do not know. My lord of Mercia thinks I shall stay with
him for many years, and marry his daughter Edith, and
when my father dies, for fathers do, in battle or in bed,
even when their sons cannot be near them, he will be
king of all England, of Mercia and Northumbria together.
His vision is even larger than my father's, who wishes to
be king only of all Northumbria. But I think they will not
have their vision, nor will I mine."

He began to sing softly, very differently than before,
a melodious chant:

"Be Thou my Vision, O Lord of my heart,
Naught is all else to me, save that Thou art.
Thou my best thought by day and by night,
Waking or sleeping, Thy presence my light.
Be Thou my Wisdom, Thou my true Word;
I ever with Thee, Thou with me, Lord.

Thou my great Father, I thy dear son;
Thou in me dwelling, I with Thee one.

Be Thou my battle-shield, sword for the fight,
Be Thou my dignity, Thou my delight.

Thou my soul's shelter, Thou my high tower;
Raise Thou me heavenward, Power of my power.

Riches I heed not or man's empty praise,
Thou mine inheritance now and always.

Thou, and Thou only, first in my heart,
High King of heaven, my treasure Thou art.

With the High King of heaven, after victory won,
May I reach heaven's joys, O Bright heaven's Sun!

Heart of my own heart, whatever befall,
Still be my Vision, O Ruler of all."

He sat so still that they sat still too, until finally Peter's foot cramped and he moved. Margery asked then in a frightened, chilled voice, "Is that your vision, Stephen, to die?"

He smiled at her, his old smile, warming her like the sun's rays, and she could not believe he meant what she thought she had heard. He shook his head. "No, Margery, indeed it is not, though we must all die, and at times I have wished to. It is a prayer I learned in Ireland, from an Irish monk, and I have never forgotten it. It is in part my vision, but I want even more." The cry in his voice, undefined, inarticulate, moved her until she wanted to take him in her arms, tall boy nearly grown that he was, and little girl that she still was.

"The world is full of visions," he said thoughtfully, "all different in some way, though some seem the same, and many of them will not allow others' visions room to have a place beside them. But I would wish for there to be a place for each of us to have our visions, like a mansion full of many rooms. But it is not possible, I think, not in the world as I know it. Vision is just what one sees with one's eyes. My vision is not for my father's warriors, for they see only one thing at a time, or theirs for me, for I must see many things, but without my father's and his warriors' visions, we shall have no world in which to have visions at all, as the world is. But I am not like my father, and I must be as I am. Once I thought I should like to be like Abbot Stephen, for whom I was named. He was the greatest man I ever knew, greater than my father, though they had something in common. Men loved him, even when he chastised them. But I do not know now. And it does not matter. I shall not have my vision, not there nor here nor anywhere."

"Why not, Stephen?" Margery asked, her heart strangely oppressed. "How can you know?"

"I have been cursed, Margery," he said with a half-smile.

"Cursed? Why, there is no such thing!"

"Once I did not think it could be true, either, but now I find I almost do. Shall I tell you? It is something that happened to me once, not just an imagining, as you think. When I went to Ireland, as I told you, I not only ate the nut of the hazel tree, which has done me little good, I took a silk embroidered cloak from an Irish poet; it was a green cloak and very beautiful and I wanted it, and so I took it. I did things sometimes like that then. Do you know what poets are, Margery?"

"I do, but I am not allowed to read them, for they write such wicked verse. There is Lord Byron, and there is Shelley, and we cannot have their books in our house."

"I do not know these names, and if you do not have the books, I suppose I shall not. Can they destroy a man?"

"I am not sure their verse is quite that strong."

"The Irish poets can. They are much feared, even by their kings, but I did not know. They can make a satire on a man, and curse him with it, if he displeases them, and that is all there is to him, he will not escape it."

"That sounds more like a witch to me than a poet," said Peter. "How do they do it?"

"They take a spear-like twig of thorn in their hand, and they go up onto a little hill, at sunrise, with the sun at their back and the morning wind in their face, and make the satire. That is all, but it is enough."

"I have never heard of anything so silly," said Peter indignantly. "You surely don't believe that."

"I hope not, but it was most impressive when I saw it."

"What was the curse then?"

He smiled and shook his head. "I could not understand the language."

"If you believed it," demanded Peter, "why did you not just kill him before he finished?"

"I did not think of that, at the time. Perhaps I should have. It would not have changed things much." He paused, as he saw the look on Margery's face. "My world is coming to an end, Margery, and they do not know it, but I do, for I have looked into the histories in your father's book room, and there is nothing of us. My father and

Aella and Penda, with their visions, are just names, or like myself, not even that, your books do not know them, and all our stories have no histories, and are lost, and Strean-aeshalch and Lindisfarne shall be destroyed, and all the monks and scholars who live within them shall be destroyed with them. Oh, God," he said, "I even know by whom, although I do not know how far away it is, and I am helpless to prevent it. Someday, perhaps, someone, scholars in another time, later than you, Margery, will learn more of us, but with our records gone, we shall be a memory, like Atlantis, and not so much as that. They will say, 'There flourished learning, there, for a time,' but what it was, and how it was, without our records, who will know?"

He did not tell her that after he had come to see her in her house, for the last time, and had said good-bye to her, he had gone expressly to her father's book room, in his desperate desire to know, or that he had seen her father, as he came out, and her father had seen him, with the tears in his eyes, and that they had talked a long while together. The sound of the books being taken out had disturbed Sir Joseph, and he had lit his candle from the tinderbox by his bed and had come downstairs in his dressing robe and slippers, with his pistol in his hand. But when he saw who it was, he had put his pistol quietly down, and led Stephen back into the book room, and they talked about his story, and the land as it was now and as it used to be. He had even showed his pistol to Stephen, when he saw Stephen did not know what it was, and explained to him its working.

A line that Sir Joseph had shown him in a new book

he had bought came now again into Stephen's mind, and it found itself on his lips: " 'Be through my lips to un-awakened earth the trumpet of a prophecy!' "

"What does that mean?" asked Margery, wide-eyed.

"Like all words, it means what it says—both more and less," he answered with a brief smile. He did not wish to tell her that her father, though kind and exceedingly interested, had asked him if, despite the historical advantages to the children, it would not be better for them all for him to stay in his own time.

"But come if you must," he had said, with his characteristic blunt honesty. "But you know now, I do see you; and that does not seem to me a good sign for either of us."

"I am going now anyway," Stephen had said, "you need not alarm yourself anymore for that. I don't think I can return. I am sorry I have vexed you."

"You have not vexed me," said Sir Joseph. "I shall be glad to see you if you come again."

The interview had grieved Stephen so, in many ways, that, absorbed in his personal grief, until this moment he had put it from his mind.

"Are you in trouble now, Stephen?" asked Margery, watching his face.

"Not really. At least, I think not. No more than my usual."

"Then why did you come? Just to see us? Can you just do that?" He shook his head.

"You called me this time, so strongly that I came."

"I did not know I did." He looked at her penetratingly. "At least, I do not think I did. At least—perhaps I did."

"I am very busy, where I am, someone is with me almost all the time, except when you are asleep. But if you want me very much, call me clearly, as you did today, and I will try to come."

"We want you all the time," protested Peter.

"That kind of wanting is not enough," said Stephen with his rarest smile. His reality suddenly left him. He seemed to slowly fade, shining like a soap bubble's colours, but imperceptibly like a fading rainbow, before their very eyes.

"I do not like for Stephen to be sad," said Peter, when he had gone.

"I do not at all," said Margery, "but I do not see what we can do about it," she said. "He lives right now in another time, though not so far from us in space. It is his time, and he must live it, I suppose. At first, I found it fun, but now I don't, for I do not see how he can ever find a way to stay here, even if he wished to. And I am not certain that he really wishes it, though he says he does. I think, though, that I shall wish it."

"Would that be fair, if he doesn't?" asked Peter with unusual perception.

"I suppose not. I must change my wish then. I must wish it only if he does, and when he does."

The Fifteenth Division

TIME PASSED, AND IN THAT TIME, AFTER SOME MONTHS, STEPHEN'S FATHER HAVING DESTROYED AELLA'S SON AND THAT REBELLION, AND SENT AEDAN RETREATING NORTH, marched South towards Mercia and Penda's castle. Penda's son received the news with shock, and moved immediately to encamp near the border in an outlying keep. There he summoned Stephen to him.

"This is not well done," he said. "If Deira, or Northumbria as he now is, thinks to deal so with me, and has so great an appetite, he will do so at the loss of you. Does he expect this?"

"I do not know what my father expects," Stephen answered whitely, torn by the not unexpected news. "He will do as he intends, and you will do with me as you see fit. But I have come to like you, even to love you, though we are enemies, and though you may not believe me, I must tell you this. My presence here will not stop him. He does not come for me, and he will not stop because of me. Though you wear me as a shield, such a shield will not make him pause in his intention."

"You have given me a thought," said Penda's son looking at him searchingly, "and it perhaps will be tried out. Do you think me a kind man, Monk's Cub, or a cruel man?"

"I think you neither, sire," answered Stephen. "You are a king, and that is a hard thing to be."

"With events as they stand now, it may be better if we speak no more together, son of Deira," said Penda's son, a little sadly. "What kindness I may feel towards you will not avail you, or persuade my cruelty to spare you."

"I know that," said Stephen, "I have never doubted it. Do not distress yourself for it. You will do as you have to do, and I see you do not believe me."

"You will stay in the quarters I have given you, son of Deira, until we move into the field, and you will allow my nephew or my son to do with you as I direct."

"I will do as you say," Stephen said, bowing his head, "but you need not fear I shall try to evade you. I was cursed long ago, and a man may not avoid his fate."

If there were tears in the eyes of anyone in the hall, there were none in Stephen's eyes, unblinded and clear-sighted. He went to his rooms, indifferent to the need others might feel for any farewells, and suffered Penda's nephew to bind his hands and his feet without protest. He lay on his bed, reviewing his life quietly before his mind, in its conflicting phases, from his earliest memories down to its present moment. What it had come to, he could not see, or any meaning in it, but if there was one, he supposed he or another would be shown it in due time. So much he had known that had moved him, and so much had appalled him. And now he was to leave it, and though they did not dream it, all these others, shortly, before a more ruthless, relentless, destroying invader than either knew how to be. He had no doubts at all about his fate. Penda's son would believe himself safe, with Stephen before him, or within his hall, and either his father would kill him regardless, or Penda's son would slay him in revenge for the broken hostage pledge, and throw his body before his father. He wondered if he would see his father's face before he died. Life was hard, he thought, but very beautiful, and suddenly, desperately, he did not want to leave it.

They came for him then, their faces averted as honourable men's faces always were, he thought, when they embark upon an action they know to be unspeakable. But to him, if he had to meet his death, it did not really matter very much if they were honourable or dishonourable, kind or cruel, ashamed or undismayed. In the end, shortly, it would all be the same to him—and to many of these very men, too. He had shown a brave indifference before Penda's son, but he no longer felt it. He felt only the most desperate desire for escape, any escape at all. There was none here for him, and he did not know where one might be. He had had so much he wanted to do, to create, to make, to express, and always he seemed to be involved only with destruction, destroying and destroyed.

He did not resist the men who bound him in front of Penda's son, who was to lead the band of men, the army, through the castle gates, and out into the field of war. He had warned them, he had even told them what his father would do, **and** they had not believed him. He could have laughed aloud, had he not felt so desperately sad for them and for his father and for himself, for most of all he wished to live and not to die. He uttered no prayers. His whole being was like a flaming prayer, burning upwards before it turned to ash and crumbled. He did not know for what to ask that might be given him, but his spirit burned, and illumined his face. He saw his father, and his father's arm uplifted, spear in hand, a few yards from him, and he saw that his father had seen him before he had seen his father. "I am still a coward," he thought. "I see my father and my king, and all I wish for is a pair of hands to cover my heart with and to pull out the spear, and I have not even that." He felt it strike him with a crashing pain and a thud of such force that it knocked Penda's son out of the saddle behind him onto the ground. He was aware that his father had pushed him hastily aside, without a glance, where he had fallen, to draw out his sword to hack the life from the fallen son of Penda. The blood from the slain man lying by him spurted out upon him and mingled with his own.

"It is fitting," he thought, "nothing is gained without a loss. He is dead, and I am dying, but I am not yet dead. I felt the pain, and I am not yet dead. That means my father cared, and it caused his aim to falter, just this once. Oh, God," he thought, "I do not want to die, here in this blood and dust, with men and horses trampling me, like a second Heavenfield; if I must die, cannot I die some other where, some other place, not here like this? Oh, God, I do not want to die at all just yet, let me not wholly die. Margery," he cried, "oh Margery, take me from this dreadful dying." He felt a terrible pain welling within him, choking him, and he saw the hooves of a warhorse rearing above him, and then, like a feather in nowhere at all, he felt himself floating away from the scene of blood and death, and dying, from the shouting and the fire. He shut his eyes, and thought, "If this is death, then I can bear it after all."

The Sixteenth and Final Division

THE CHILDREN SAW THE BALLOON SOAR OVER THEIR SUM-
MER HOUSE, PULLED UPWARDS BY A DRAFT, AND RUSHING
FORWARD, THEY WATCHED IT FLOAT MAJESTICALLY TOWARDS
the lake, its many-coloured stripes and bands shimmering
in the sunlight. With a common consent, without a word,
they followed it. They met Joseph arriving in the gig in
a state of excitement, who informed them that there was
no one in the balloon. He had been to see the launching,
he said, and the descent. The engineer and the balloonist
had both dismounted from the basket and were adjusting
the ballast and preparing to secure it fast, when a sudden
rush of wind had seized the balloon and torn the ropes
out of their grasp, and tossed it back into the upper air.
They had stood watching it helplessly as it rocketed its
way jauntily upwards, rocking softly back and forth, like
a child loosed on holiday. Now they were all following
it, he said, to find out where it would choose finally to
descend, in order to recover it.

"It may never come down!" cried Peter excitedly.

"Oh, it will do that," said Joseph patronisingly from his superior height in the gig and his superior knowledge.

"How do you know?" The balloon looked very high to them, and seemed to be going higher, despite the dip over their house.

"The balloonist says so. Either the gas will leak out slowly, or a change in temperature will cause it to burst."

"I'm glad there's no one in it. Look! It has turned away from the lake, and is going towards the fields."

"I can see it more clearly," said Margery. "Is it coming down?" Her heart seemed arrested by the beautiful sphere, and a sudden emotion she did not understand. She began to run towards it.

"Hi!" cried Joseph. "It will be miles away before it descends. I will take you in the gig."

Margery shook her head, and continued to run, compelled towards it, straight across the fields, clambering over the stone walls, and the stick fences, cross-country as the gig could not go. Peter, obedient as always to Margery's impulses, expressed or unexpressed, followed afterward, as fast as his shorter but stronger legs might take him. He caught up with her, panting and blowing.

"Something has happened to it," he said more excitedly than before but with no breath left over for exclamation. "It is coming down, and it is coming down fast. Lord!" he cried. "Look! It is going to land two fields over, maybe in Sir Francis' field."

"Don't say *Lord*, Peter," said Margery automatically, her eyes fixed on the balloon rapidly reapproaching earth. She began to run again, and Peter followed her. They saw other people converging on the same spot towards which they had directed themselves.

They followed the balloon, running with the crowd, to the field where it fell. There was already a ring of people around it, but they pushed their way through. The balloon had caught a tree and ripped away, and fallen over a wattle fence, the sharp cross-edged fence spikes poking through the cloth. The basket, which should have been empty, had turned over, and lay across a figure that already hands were uncovering.

"There's someone in it," the children heard voices saying.

"There's someone there now, and he's in fancy dress, it must be the University students having a party and a prank."

"Then they should have the law on them, disturbing the peace and stealing baskets."

"I think he's hurt, the basket's bloody on the side," exclaimed another, eyes riveted in eager horror.

"Lor! He has fallen on the fence and it has hurt his chest," a woman cried, and she turned green and came over faint. Part of the crowd left the balloonist and clustered about her. A man, a farmer's herd, walked up to the figure, now uncovered, and looked at the gaping, bleeding wound, and turned his head, and was sick. A parting in the crowd enabled the children to see the figure lying on the ground.

"It is Stephen," Margery cried.

At that moment her childhood left her. She dropped Amanda underfoot, and ran across the space that separated her, careening desperately into the obstacles that blocked her path. Peter ran interference for her ahead of her, zig-zagging, his head lowered effectively like a cannon ball. She knelt beside the familiar figure, dismayed by the terrible wound but in no way fainting. She took her shawl and covered him with it.

"Is he dead?" asked Peter.

"I don't know. Peter, you must run as fast as you can, and find Father, and Mother too, if you can, but find Father first. I do not know what to do. Oh, Peter, have you any breath left? Oh, run, Peter!"

"This is my cousin Stephen," she explained to the startled faces, inquisitive, angry, interfering, perplexed, helpful, that surrounded her. "Has anyone gone for a doctor? Does anyone know if one lives here?" She saw a man nod and disengage himself from the crowd. She did not know what he said, but she supposed he was leaving to fetch one. "He is so cold," she said. "What can I cover him with? My scarf is not enough. I will buy it all from you if the blood on the ground spoils it." She waited, her face expectant, while various shawls and a riding coat were found, and a woman left to find blankets from her cottage in the next field. She watched them lift him slightly off the ground, to place him on the blankets, and though he was not heavy, she realised from their motions that he had weight. The significance was not lost on her.

"He is going to stay," she realised, speaking to herself. Or had he come only to die? And why? She put her hand in his, and it fell limply, a dead weight—with weight, what Stephen had always lacked.

"You will not die, Stephen," she said fiercely under her breath. "I will not let you. And you must not let yourself."

He opened his eyes, from somewhere a long way away, and looked at her. They were frightened, and flecked with blood, and glazing, but they were still Stephen's eyes. "I do not wish to," he said faintly. "Help me, Margery," he said, and closed his eyes again. But he held fast to her hand that she put in his.

She stayed there protectively until Peter and her father made their way back across the fields. Peter had not had to go far, for he had found Sir Joseph in the high field already. He had noticed the balloon, and he had thought to see it too.

"What will you do with Stephen?" she cried anxiously, "I am sure he did not mean to steal the balloon, and he is hurt."

Sir Joseph saw she did not understand the implications of Stephen's appearance, and he did not enlighten her. "Peter, you must find Joseph. I shall send Joseph in the gig to fetch the doctor, if he does not come quickly. I should like to remove him myself if we can make a stretcher, before anyone arrives to announce the balloon was empty. He is hurt too badly for me to hurt him any worse." He began giving quick orders to the most sensible-looking of the persons around him, about wattles, and he saw the approaching arrival of Sir Francis and the doctor with relief.

"Will Stephen die?" asked Margery anxiously, her eyes on his white face.

"I would say he was dead already, except he does not seem to be," said Sir Joseph absently, his mind on the details of the removal.

"Stephen, Stephen," whispered Margery. "Stephen, you are here. Come back. We will take care of you, and you will be safe. Stephen," she whispered, "it is Margery."

He opened his eyes, clouded with past anguish, and looked at her, and smiled, and then he closed them again.

"There is spunk in your boy, Margery," said Sir Joseph. "We will pull him through, if we can. I shall send Joseph to London as soon as we reach the house, to fetch a second surgeon as well."

"Do you realise, Sir Joseph," said the country surgeon, when they were all finally situated in a bedroom in the house, "that this is not a fence wound, as you said? It is made by a spear, or a very large sword."

"Yes, I saw that," said Sir Joseph, "but I did not see any reason to mention it, since we don't know how he came by it. What can I do about it? Isn't the first thing to see if he will live?"

"I suppose so," said the doctor, "but I am not an army surgeon."

"I am having one fetched. Do the best you can until he comes," said Sir Joseph with both severity and encouragement in his command.

It appeared, after several days, no one quite knowing or understanding why, that Stephen would live to laugh over his strange descent. But when he finally woke, for any length of time, he did not know them. He looked at them blankly, and their faces were clearly those of strangers to him. Margery was shocked. She did not know what she had envisioned, but she had not envisioned that he would return to them with no knowledge of them or himself.

"His personal self may return when he is stronger," Sir Joseph comforted her, "and if he is to stay here, it is best he not remember what must have happened to him or how he came here."

"But how is Stephen here, and still not here at all?" she asked, bewildered, and not understanding.

"His memory is gone. The surgeon says that sometimes happens. It seems sad to you, but it is kinder, Margery, that Stephen not remember, and it will be better for you if you forget."

"I shall never forget," said Margery, wondering a little even as she said it.

"To live in two worlds," her father said, attempting to explain and to comfort her, "and in two times, cannot be done by anyone for long. Surely you can see that, Margery. I would not have believed it could be done at all. I wish I knew, though, who it was that hurt him." In a way they did not understand, although they guessed a part of it, Stephen had died to his own world in a bitter ending, how bitter they would not know, and he would not be able to tell them. But Margery and Peter did know, for Stephen had told them, that in his own time the wounded did not survive, certainly not with the wound he had. The aim of the sender had faltered by only a hair's-breadth, and it was a tax for the London surgeon's skill to recover him from it.

"He tried to come to us, as it happened, don't you think?" Margery said to Peter. "Do you think I helped? He liked us once before. Don't you think when he knows us, he will like us again?"

He did not even look like Stephen anymore, Margery thought. His hair, that had fallen to his shoulders, had been cut to Joseph's length, some inches shorter, and he was wearing one of Joseph's nightshirts. "But it is Stephen's face," she reassured herself, his lips, his nose—"or are they Joseph's too?" she thought, suddenly struck by the resemblance as they lay, immobile, without their particular informing personality. When he was quite well again, she thought, his eyes would be Stephen's again, and the lips would smile as Stephen's had, even if he did not know them. She did not believe Stephen's particular spirit would disappear, even if his memory had, for he had forgotten many things during his previous visits. He had liked them as strangers, and he would surely like them as strangers a second time.

It was weeks, however, before any trace at all of the Stephen she had known reappeared. They had left the lake, their return already long delayed, as soon as Stephen's condition permitted him to be moved again, and returned to the house where Stephen had first met them. He had been obedient and done all that was requested of him, but he lay mainly with his eyes closed, and even when he was able to leave his bed and walk hesitantly and stumblingly about in his weakness, he seemed to be more sleepwalking than awake. She went with him on short walks on the terrace, and later she sat by him as he sunbathed on the winter lawn or in the solarium, ready and waiting to perform any errand he might wish, but he did not seem to know she was there, or to know who brought him flowers and fruit as offerings on his table.

"Margery is like a Faithful Hound," said Peter intuitively, "and if Stephen doesn't give her a pat on the head soon, she will die of unrequited devotion."

He was mistaken, though, in Margery's capacity for patient unrewarded service. She was not discouraged, or cast down, or even expectant. But she was like the Faithful Hound Peter described, in that she did require only to be with Stephen, having found him again, even if he had not found himself. She resented only the times when necessity, hers or his, forced her from his side.

"You will take roots, Margery," said Peter. "Come and play!" She shook her head. "Stephen does not even want you."

"I do want her," said a voice they knew, right beside them.

"Oh, Stephen," cried Margery, and she began all at once to cry.

"Don't be a watering pot," exclaimed Peter crossly, feeling he might turn into one himself. Stephen smiled appreciatively at a word that stirred some reminiscence he could not recapture. He did not pursue the effort.

"You are Margery?" he asked tentatively. She nodded, blinking back her tears. "And I am Stephen?" She nodded again. He did not question how she knew. He repeated the name again, to himself, firmly, as though he liked the sound: "Stephen."

"Papa says there is a word like *Steven*, that means a voice. I am glad to hear your voice. You have been asleep, Stephen. Have you been dreaming?"

He shook his head. "I remember nothing, not even any dream. Do I know you?" She nodded. "Have I known you long?" She nodded her head again simply, not trying to explain the complications there. "How strange. I do not remember you at all." He looked at her face. "Oh, I have hurt you."

"No," she said, "I do not mind, Stephen. You cannot help it. I am just glad you have come back."

"Are you my sister?" he asked.

"No, I am not, I am just Margery."

"Is Sir Joseph my father?"

"No, he is mine."

He looked at her suddenly and smiled, and he said, "I am glad you are not my sister, Margery," but he did not explain himself. He leaned back and closed his eyes, tired again. He did not say any more, for a long time, and she thought he had fallen asleep again. His voice again startled her, for his voice was as it had always been.

"What is to become of me, Margery, if Sir Joseph is not my father, and this is not my family, and this lovely house and garden is not my home?"

"My father thinks you may be related to us in some way, though not very nearly," she added. "You did not live so very far away from us, once."

"Don't you know—*cousin* Margery?"

"It does not matter. We love you just as you are, and for yourself."

He did not answer, but he lay back, regarding her, his eyes like deep pools.

"I love you, too, Margery. I don't know why, but I remember that I do. You are a very little girl."

"Not so very little, now, and I will grow," she said smiling, her dimple suddenly appearing. They looked at each other, quietly, and she put her hand in his, and he put his other over it. It was an affirmation that they both understood, but they did not speak of it.

"What, then, is to become of me?" Stephen asked again.

"You are to stay here, and do just as you like, until you are quite fit again. Then my father will send you to Oxford, or wherever you like, to prepare for what you want to do."

"Oxford?" he asked.

"That is a place with books, Stephen, where one learns how to do what one needs to do. At least, my father thinks it is the place where you will learn it."

"Why should he do this? Haven't you other brothers and sisters?"

"Yes, I do. You are very special to us, Stephen. He will do it because he wants to, he does not need any other reason."

The boy that was Stephen looked at her with a sudden quick smile of gratitude, shy for the first time and vulnerable in his new life.

"How old am I, Margery?" he asked, with awakening curiosity. "I cannot tell myself. I feel immensely old, but I do not seem to take up much space."

"You are sixteen, Stephen. Today is St. Stephen's Day, and my father says it is your birthday." She was laughing and crying at one time, her tears and her smiles mingled like the snow and the rain falling together outside the window.

"Then yesterday was Christmas," he said, his memory stirring faintly, "and I did not know it. Was it merry?"

"It is merrier today," she said.

"And you know who I am, Margery?"

"A little. Not entirely."

"Will you tell me someday when I am stronger? I do not really want to know now."

"Perhaps," she said. "Let's wait and see."

Epilogue

Now read Alfred's preface to his translation of The Pastoral Care, written after the Danish invasions, in the year A.D. 894, or near that year, in Wessex:

Ælfred kyning hateð gretan Wærferð biscep his wordum
Alfred, king, bids greet Waerforth, bishop, with these
luflice ond freondlice; ond ðe cyðan hate ðæt me com swiðe
words, lovingly and friendly, and I bid make known to you
oft on gemynd, hwelce wiotan iu wæron giond Angelcynn,
that it comes to me very often in mind, what wise men were
ægðer ge godcundra hada ge woruldcundra; ond hu gesæliglica
formerly throughout England, both of the divine ranks and
tida ða wæron giond Angelcynn; ond hu ða kyningas ðe ðone
the secular; and how happy and blessed were the times then
onwald hæfdon ðæs folces on ðam dagum Gode ond his ærend-
throughout England; and how then the kings who held the
authority of the people in those days obeyed God and his
wrecum hersumedon; ond hu hie ægðer ge hiora sibbe ge hiora
messengers; and how they held peace and morals and authority
siodo ge hiora onweald innanbordes gehioldon, ond eac
within their borders, and how they also extended their

ut hiora eðel gerymdon; ọnd hu him ða speow ægðer ge
territory outside of them; and how they succeeded both
mid wige ge mid wisdome; ọnd eac ða godcundan hadas hu
with war and with wisdom; and also how eager the divine
giorne hie wæron ægðer ge ymb lare ge ymb liornunga, ge
ranks were both about learning and about teaching, and
ymb ealle ða ðiowotdomas ðe hie Gode don scoldon; ọnd hu
about all the services which they ought to do for God; and
man utanbordes wisdom ọnd lare hieder on lọnd sohte, ọnd hu
how a man abroad would seek for wisdom and learning hither
we hie nu sceoldan ute begietan, gif we hie habban sceoldon.
in the land; and how we now must get these things outside, if
Swæ clæne hio wæs oðfeallenu on Angelcynne ðæt swiðe feawa
we should have them. So clean it was fallen off in England
wæron behionan Humbre ðe hiora ðeninga cuðen understọndan on
that there were very few on this side of the Humber who could
Ẹnglisc oððe furðum an ærendgewrit of Lædene on Ẹnglisc
understand their services in English or even translate
arẹccean; ọnd ic wene ðætte noht mọnige begiondan Humbre
into English a letter from out of Latin; and I think that
næren. Swæ feawa hiora wæron ðæt ic furðum anne anlepne ne
there were not many beyond the Humber. So few of them there
maeg geðẹncean be suðan Tẹmese, ða ða ic to rice feng. Gode
were that I am not able to think of even a single one south
of the Thames, at the time when I received the sovereignty.
ælmihtegum sie ðọnc ðætte we nu ænigne onstal habbað lareowa.
Thanks be to God Almighty that we now have any supply of teachers.
Ọnd for ðon ic ðe bebiode ðæt ðu do swæ ic geliefe ðæt ðu
And for this I bid you that you do as I believe you will, that you
wille, ðæt ðu ðe ðissa woruldðinga to ðæm geæmetige, swæ ðu
so free yourself from worldly matters as you oftenest may, that
oftost mæge, ðæt ðu ðone wisdom ðe ðe God sealde ðær ðær ðu
there where you may put in safekeeping the wisdom which God gave
hiene befæstan mæge, befæste. Geðẹnc hwelc witu us ða becomon for

you, that you do put it. Think what punishments may come to us then
ðisse worulde, ða ða we hit nohwæðer ne selfe ne lufodon,
for this world, when we neither loved it for itself,
ne eac oðrum monnum ne lefdon: ðone naman anne we lufodon ðætte
nor even left it for other men: we loved the name alone that we
we Cristne wæren, ond swiðe feawe ða ðeawas.
were Christians, and very few of the uses.
Ða ic ða ðis eall gemunde, ða gemunde ic eac hu ic geseah, ær
ðæm ðe hit eall forhergod wære ond forbærned, hu ða ciricean
Then when I was mindful of all this, then I remembered also
how I saw before that it was all laid waste and burned, how the
churches stood throughout all England, filled with treasures and
giond eall Angelcynn stodon maðma ond boca gefylda, ond eac micel
books, and also a great multitude of God's servants; and they knew
menigeo Godes ðiowa; ond ða swiðe lytle fiorme ðara boca wiston, for
very little benefit of those books because they might not understand
ðæm ðe hie hiora nanwuht ongietan ne meahton, for ðæm ðe hie næron
them at all, for they were not written in their own language. Thus
on hiora agen geðiode awritene. Swelce hie cwæden: "Ure ieldran,
they might have spoken: "Our elders, when they formerly held these
ða ðe ðas stowa ær hioldon, hie lufodon wisdom, ond ðurh ðone
places, they loved wisdom, and through it they found wealth,
hie begeaton welan, ond us læfdon. Her mon mæg giet gesion
and left it to us. Here a man may yet see their footprint, but
hiora swæð, ac we him ne cunnon æfter spyrigean, ond for ðæm
we may not follow after them; and for this reason we have now
we habbað nu ægðer forlæten ge ðone welan ge ðone wisdom, for
lost both the wealth and the wisdom, because we would not in-
ðæm ðe we noldon to ðæm spore mid ure mode onlutan." . . .
cline to the footprint with our mind." . . .